ROOT and SHOOT

ROOT and SHOOT

Flash and Short Fiction by

NATHAN LESLIE

*t*P
Texture Press
2015

Published in the United States by
Texture Press
1108 Westbrooke Terrace
Norman, OK 73072

For ordering information,
visit the Texture Press website at
www.texturepress.org

ISBN-13: 978-0-692-52048-2
ISBN-10: 0-692-52048-1

Table of Contents

Acknowledgements

Big thanks goes to Arlene Ang and Mark Worthington for the wonderful design and cover of this book (as well as internal photos), respectively. I would also like to thank Julie Leslie, who puts up with me on an hourly basis. Also big thanks to CL Bledsoe, Charles Rammelkamp, Tara Masih and Jen Michalski, among many others, for their writerly support.

I'd like to thank the following magazines for initially publishing stories from this collection:

--*Boulevard* for "A Sunday Story"
--*Cimarron Review* for "La Isla de Cangrejos"
--*Sierra Nevada College Review* for "Passing"
--*Shenandoah* for "Hickory Hollow"
--*Gargoyle* for "Let's Do Thai," "The Make Out Club,"
  "The Miniaturist" and "In Different Rooms"
--*Red Rock Review* for "Hatchling" and "Whipped"
--*Word Riot* for "Laser Eye"
--*Ghoti* for "Leisure"
--*Per Contra* for "A Mound"
--*The Potomac* for "Night Teaching" and "Status Quo"
--*JMWW* for "Pickle Man"
--*Elimae* for "New Cycle"
--*Hobart* for "Pastry Chef"
--*Scribble* for "Upholstery"
--*Plains Review* for "Respect the Process"

--*Big Lucks Literary Journal* for "Upgrade"

--*Shady Side Review* for "Indigo"

--*Birmingham Arts Journal* for "Behind Me"

--*Offcourse* for "Backless"

--*Word Riot* for "Laser Eye"

--*Abbeywood Press Anthology* for "Leisure"

--*Stepaway Magazine* for "The Walker"

--*Slow Trains* for "Stained Glass"

1. SNAPSHOTS

By the Lake

At eighty-one my mother is beginning to lose her memory. She still has my name down but now believes my brother, Bobby, lives in Santa Cruz, California. Bobby has never lived in California; I'm not sure he's ever *been* to California. Since 1983 he has lived abroad in various locations. My mother is still a beautiful woman. She possesses piercing blue eyes the exact color of the Caribbean, and long angular features with high, sharp cheek bones. Somehow the white cable-knit sweaters, to which she is partial, bring her beauty out even more.

Mother is back at the cabin—tending to the dishes, sweeping the porch. She claims she enjoys these simple tasks. Still, she's taxing. I know the next few years of my life will consist of helping her in every aspect of her life, family maintenance to say the least. Bobby is obviously useless.

I'm standing by the edge of the lake behind my uncle, who smells faintly of burnt onions. He stands in front of the ladder rails, arms on hips as if he were the lifeguard. Two women I've never seen before recline on the concrete pier on identical, white towels. In lieu of sand, raised concrete slabs ring the lake and protrude over the water. From a pragmatist's standpoint I can understand this. However, it makes for a grim scene, especially on a foggy day like today. The sun is a flashlight through milk.

Set back from the edge of the water, one of the women reads, her left hip rising from the concrete prominently. She wears a beige swimming cap and for just a moment I think she's bald. She's reading something by Agatha Christie, smiling to herself. The woman on the right sits in a triangular position, a small red beach chair propping her up. Aside from the two horizontal, orange stripes on my uncle's black swim trunks the chair provides the only splash of color. The other woman turns her head, watching my uncle standing there. She wears white-rimmed, oversized sunglasses made popular by Hollywood starlets trying to cloak themselves from the paparazzi. The combination of the coaster-sized sunglass lenses and the woman's permed chestnut hair give her resemblance to a lost backup singer for Ike Turner. I've never seen either woman before, and given the space between them they clearly don't know each other well—or don't want to. They don't speak. They don't exchange eye contact.

I suddenly have an urge to dive from the edge of the platform into the lake. I realize if I get a running start and jump away from the edge, it's doable. This is what the kids do—dive straight in. We've been vacationing at the lake for decades.

My uncle rotates his torso back to me and winks. Jim still treats me as if I am a little girl, though I'm going gray myself these days. He is kind and generous and lonely. The three of us—my mother, my uncle, me—make for a sad-sack combination. Forty-two, divorced, single, and childless: my life is not what I imagined it would be. It isn't what I would have wanted, either. I'm just living it, trying to find my way.

"Getting in?"

"You bet," I say. I kick off my flip-flops, and stare out over what I can see of the horizon. My bones ache and my muscles ache even more. Yet, I long for the cold, clammy water. I want to be startled by something. I want to pare down to the basic elements.

As I jump I can feel grit and dirt beneath my toes. The air is motionless, even as I run through it. I feel as if moving through a vacuum. As I reach the edge of the platform, I cast my body through the air. Floating, I focus on remembering everything I can. The baked smell lingering on my father, my mother's smile, rolling in the clover and dandelion, making love for the first time, the squeak of my own violin, painting my bathroom walls, the click of my fingers on a calculator.

Then I hit the cold water and I am in it, nosing downward. I open my eyes and am suffused with lambent light. I am surrounded by silt. My body knows what to do. It rights itself. I curl up to the light, toward what remains of it in the fog above the jostling waves.

In Different Rooms

I don't care what Gerry says, I'm not sitting on the aluminum eggs in our plastic "nest" in ninety five plus degree heat. Everyone has a limit, and that's mine. I'm still a man after all. Or despite it.

Patty's tail swishes along the pavement, kicking up sand and grit. I brush against her with my thick leg scales and she hisses with her forked prosthetic tongue. Melodramatically, if you ask me. I don't know if Iguanas even *have* forked tongues, but Patty says we're supposed to be basilisks. Neither one hisses as far as I know. This is our argument: Iguanas, basilisks; basilisks, iguanas. Gerry won't say, or doesn't know. I suspect the latter.

"What?" I say.

"You know," Patty says.

I hiss with my forked prosthetic tongue.

"It's not time yet," I say. I know why she is pressing, but I don't care. "We have to wait until after one o'clock."

My leg scales are different than my arm scales. My leg scales are plate-like, while my arm scales are thin and pointier. Patty's have a bluish tinge, mine a greenish tinge. We must consider the possibility that *she* is the basilisk and I'm the iguana. We just can't reproduce is all. Interspecies, and all that.

I don't know why Gerry has us in the Staples parking lot, of all places. We usually get Old Navy, L.L. Bean, Britches—stores where perhaps customers can purchase items made from what we represent, or at least our genus. Lizard wallets, watch bands, belts, lizard scarves, I don't know. Not sure about basilisk products. The connection always seemed tenuous to me.

Today the yuppies on lunch break are looking at us as if we are nudists dangling our naughty bits in their children's applesauce, which frankly would be far more comfortable. What lizards have to do with fax machines I haven't the slightest. We're getting seventy five for the day, same as two months prior. So be it.

Living paycheck to paycheck isn't part of the American dream. At least mine. We both know this. However, it's a trade off. Ever since we broached the idea of divorce we decided we'd rather work out our problems together than separate. It's not a moral question. It's a practical one. Who wants to go through unwanted turmoil? Isn't one person essentially as good as another? If not, what's the real difference? Isn't compromise easier than starting from scratch?

Our solution? Working together. We tried food service—too grueling. We tried sales—too slick. We tried construction—too "hammers and nails." Still, all of these were better than a blunted relationship, living in different rooms. Albeit, we only have three rooms—they are still different. Recently it's been Animal Pursuits. That's what Gerry calls it. He's got mongoose (mongeese?), eagles, cows and bulls, pumas, and us—team lizard.

And it's not as if we have stopped at sharing work. We decided to invest some time in hobbies, also. We did improvisational comedy classes (we weren't funny); we tried ceramics (too messy); we tried patio gardening (the plants died); writing groups (we didn't understand the significance of "trope" and "archetype").

In short, we're trying to revive our relationship. We are lucky—no tragedies to speak of. None of this maudlin BS you read in those novels featuring some gauzy image of a couple embracing haphazardly on a rose-bush-strewn cliff overlooking the crashing surf at sunset. Our two year old wasn't run over by a tractor trailer. Didn't die of kiddie cancer or something. We just became preoccupied with other matters. That was then. This is now.

At one o'clock we duck behind the Staples Dumpster, sit on the curb and scarf down our Jerry's subs despite the fact the bread tastes faintly medicinal (I try my best not to think about the Gerry-Jerry connection). Perhaps the pickles are tainted. As I'm eating my "side-dish" (Sun Chips) and sucking down my lukewarm Sprite, a passing thought occurs to me: I wonder what it might be like to make love wearing lizard outfits. *That* could bring us even closer, I think. Something has to give.

As we eat, a resplendent Pakistani mother and her pre-teen daughter walk by through the alley-like passage between Staples and the adjacent Kids-R-Us. This surprises both of us. The girl stares at our fast food and scrunches her brow.

"Do real lizards eat chips?"

I shrug and hiss at her.

"Shouldn't you be in school?" I say.

"She had a dentist appointment," her mother says, picking up the pace.

"Uh-huh," I say. Now I'm wondering if lizard mating is really in the cards after all. I need to do some mood maintenance.

As we stand out there in the parking lot, gesticulating and crouching like we think lizards might, I hum "Message in a Bottle," slapping my plastic scales at the appropriate time. Patty's favorite song (not sure exactly why). I can feel the eyes. They stare. Children cry.

"Are we really going to stick this thing out?" Patty says.

I keep humming. She probes me with her pointy, clawed fingers.

"Sure," I say. "Why not?"

"I'm just saying…"

"We can put out a request for mongeese," I say. I heard they get the furniture stores. I'm imagining possible twenty percent discounts. We could use a new dresser and a love seat.

"No, I mean *all* this animal stuff," she says. "These shitty jobs. Can't we do better for ourselves?" I watch a guy in a burgundy pinstriped suit hustle into Staples with a shopping list. "How much further?"

I know what she means. We both do. There is such a thing as overdoing it. I shrug, and speed up the pace of my hissing and writhing. We are former anthropology majors. There's gotta be something for us out there. Even data entry would be acceptable.

"Let's quit then," I say. She looks at me, throws up her hands as if to say, "Okay, then what?" I do the same.

"Fine," she says.

"Let's wait until after tomorrow though," I say.

"Why?"

Then I know it's in the works. I can see it all unfold. We drive home in full lizard regalia. We run up the four flights of stairs to our apartment. We kick back Billy-Bob, shut him in the bathroom with his Nine Lives and his shit box. We kneel down on the unmapped kitchen floor, hissing and clawing at each other, raking at each other's scales. I bend her over, just like animals do. Exactly like that.

A Mound

Ethan's black Crown Vic is streaked with mud, the pattern resembling the Milky Way or the fumes from a jet plane. He feels pathetic, thinks of that line from Thoreau: "The mass of men lead lives of quiet desperation." Ethan always liked the one about stereotyped despair lurking beneath heightened entertainment even better. He can't recall exactly how it goes. Ethan thinks paraphrasing is a sign of sloppiness, but he is unable even to do that.

Ethan sips acrid gas-station coffee from a stained Styrofoam cup, sits on his hood. He's waiting for the clouds to part, for the sun to reappear. Ethan crosses his arms, pulls on another taupe J. Crew sweater, scratches at his four-day-old stubble. For a minute he feels he's roughing it. It's colder than Ethan would like for mid-Spring, also prettier. His stomach tightens.

Aside from the greasy Southern food, Ethan doesn't mind staying in small towns like Franklin. He can drive around these mountains all day. Wayah Bald, Tanasee Bald, Richard Balsam—bring it on.

The beginning of enjoying himself rests in not exactly knowing why he's here. He is happily married, or considers himself to be so. He calls Nancy each evening. Their daughter, Madison, coos into the phone. Ethan just wanted some alone time to drive the land, take pictures, breathe the outer Smokies—the mountains away from the tourist traps of Gatlinburg and Cherokee and Bryson City and Fontana Village. The drives afford him views he didn't think he'd find—offbeat antique shops and junkyards and construction cones and roadside dives and trailer parks. Ethan is a tourist, an outsider. There is actually something comforting about this. It allows him to take the pressure off himself. Ethan is a bureaucrat for the CDA. He doesn't reap pleasure from his job exactly. It's not gratifying, but who said work has to be?

Unfolding the North Carolina map, Ethan peers at the route from Franklin to Tamassee. Yesterday he drove from Turtletown to Suit to Murphy to Marble, Andrews, Aquone and then, finally, over to Wayah Bald. These names just roll off his tongue: Ethan almost *feels* like a Southerner by the simple act of uttering them. Today he wants to head down through Cullasaja, Gneiss, and stop at Bridal Veil Falls and Whiteside Mountain. Then, just for kicks, he thinks he will head down across the Georgia line into Dillard and Mountain City and Clayton and back up through Hiawassee. Chatuge Lake looks like it might be a decent respite. The names.

He will lounge on a dock by the lake and watch the birds and the budding trees and then find a place to stay in Hayesville just north of the line, and he will find something to eat before he calls Nancy from the butt end of his motel bed. Ethan has never been one to mind a plan. He could plot out each and every day and would be happy to follow along, reveling in a sense of completion.

Bridal Veil Falls is lovely, and once he drives down the road, Ethan feels fortunate to almost immediately find a hiking trail for Whiteside Mountain. As he drives up an incline on a narrow back spur Ethan spots a young man sitting on the asphalt, a briefcase clenched in one hand. Afraid to swerve around him, Ethan stops the car twenty yards away and lets the car idle. The man's other hand is entrenched firmly in his pocket. Ethan is worried the man has a gun or a knife, though the man is dressed in a black business coat and Ethan can clearly see a red tie poking out from the monochrome. Ethan doesn't know if he should beep his horn or get out of the car and speak to the guy. He doesn't want a confrontation, but on the other hand, he doesn't want to make his way around him: Ethan is worried the man's suicidal urges will force him to throw himself in the way of the car. A mere attempt at escape could spring the worst-case scenario.

Ethan pulls to the far right side of the road and cuts the engine. He realizes that this is the more intelligent decision: if there is a tussle he wouldn't want the young man to steal his car. Ethan doesn't feel comfortable. He flips his cell phone, places it in the pocket of his fleece jacket for safe measure. Ethan wishes he had a baseball bat with which he could defend himself, if it came to that. Something to help him feel at ease.

Instead, Ethan approaches the man with palms outstretched, in a mollifying manner.

"You okay there?" Ethan says, walking slowly toward the man.

The young man's gold-rimmed glasses catch the sun. The horseshoe pattern of leaves around the man's head is a brilliant green, and pink and white flowers speckle the background. Ethan thinks the man can't be any older than twenty-three. He is baby-faced and his hair is parted neatly and his Adam's apple bobs on his thin neck.

"Oh yeah," he says, popping up with an ironic smirk. "I was just meditating really. Resting. It's quiet."

"Right in the middle of the road?" Ethan drops his hands.

"Sure, it's not often someone comes up here anyway."

Ethan looks up the road. He can see other houses. He can hear a dog barking in the distance. He's not inclined to believe the guy's account, at least that's what Ethan's gut tells him.

"Are you heading out to work?" Ethan says. "Do you need a lift?"

"No, I'm not getting in the car with someone I don't know," the man says. "If that's what you mean. It's just one of those things to me." He doesn't seem to have an accent. Ethan snorts in laughter, and then laughs. He laughs one notch too hard and it feels bogus.

"What? What is it?" the young man says.

Ethan finds the guy's principled stance on strangers humorous since *he* is a stranger.

"Never mind," Ethan says. Ethan pivots to return to his car. He's ready to drive up the road to Whiteside Mountain. The man in the tie shouts, "Hey." After the initial exchange, this startles Ethan. Ethan looks over his shoulder. The young man's expression has changed, stiffened, pursed. He looks sullen, his face drained.

"Let me show you something," the man says. He begins walking off to the right through a patch of saplings and through the woods. The man doesn't turn around to see if Ethan is following and Ethan watches the young man walk as he carries his briefcase with one stiff arm. After a moment's deliberation Ethan can't help himself: he follows.

"My name is Chuck," the man says, still walking. He still doesn't turn around. He's walking straight ahead, shoulders slightly hunched. At his collar, Chuck's hair tapers down to a point. Something about it reminds Ethan of duck feathers. Underfoot twigs snap, leaves shuffle. Through the gaps in the trees Ethan watches the clouds scud by. The air has warmed, grown humid. One thing Ethan loves about the spring is the utter lack of insects. He has factored this into his thinking.

They walk through the woods in this way, up an incline, and after a few minutes the path leads into an opening. Over Chuck's shoulder Ethan can see a rusty chain-link fence, a green shed, a column of azaleas. They walk toward it. Chuck leads Ethan around to the left and opens the gate and they walk into the muddy yard. Ethan wonders if a dog is to blame, perhaps a goat.

Sitting in the exact middle of the yard is a small mound of snow, maybe three feet in diameter. The mound of snow is gray and brown around the edges and the mound's crest is streaked with mud. It looks like a miniature mountain, a train model of a mountain. Ethan wonders if it was once a base for a snowman.

"Look at that, would you?" Chuck says. "It's May and it still hasn't melted. Isn't that something?"

Ethan nods and shrugs. "That's the way it goes sometimes, isn't it?" Ethan feels tentative, hackneyed. Strangers. "Snow does last longer than we think sometimes."

"Not sure what that means," Chuck says. He stands behind the snow mound, one hand in his coat pocket, the other hand still holding the brief case.

"Is this what you wanted to show me?"

"I mean it must be one cold mound, isn't it? Yeah, do you see any other snow around?"

"No," Ethan says. Now that he thinks of it he hasn't.

"That's right. It's some kind of special snow. It's symbolic."

Ethan isn't sure what to say. He doesn't want to disappoint the guy, but on the other hand he doesn't want to lie to him. Ethan guesses the snow mound hasn't melted as a result of the insulating mud. At least, if he had to wager, this is what he'd wager on. He decides to err on the side of politeness and refrain from saying anything. Looking at a mound of dirty snow isn't his idea of entertainment or deep meaning. He's ready to get back to his car, hike up a mountain.

"You live here," Ethan says.

"Yeah," Chuck says, stiff as a rod. "But there's this thing..." Chuck's voice trails off. He looks at the mound of snow, as if it is about to speak to him. His eyes widen. "I'm quitting medical school. It's just.... Well, I did already. Today actually."

"Oh," Ethan says. He isn't sure what to say.

"Yeah, you got it right—I'm volunteering. Iraq. I mean, I just figure there's more need for me there. Or Afghanistan if that's where they want me. I don't care."

"Oh," Ethan says. This isn't what he expected, but by the odd way the guy has been acting Ethan thinks this makes an odd kind of sense. He just doesn't know what to do, what to say. Through the trees Ethan can see a white, ramshackle Victorian-era house. It looks abandoned. A gathering of crows lands on the cupola, squawks.

"Yeah, it's nothing my father wants me to do. My mother's gone, and I'm here. He needs me and all. But I figure..." Chuck's voice trails off again. He cocks his head, twists his neck, withdraws his free hand and massages the back of his neck. Chuck stares back into the mound of snow, this time as if in it he might find an answer to the world's problems. "I don't know," he says. "I didn't get more than an hour of sleep last night. My head is fuzzy."

Ethan watches Chuck watching the snow and he kicks at a muddy stick in the muddy yard. He listens to the chortling crows. They stand like that for a while. Ethan thinks of things he might say, but he doesn't say them. Platitudes only. There is nothing to say.

Ethan realizes he wouldn't say them even if Chuck were his brother or father or best friend. There is nothing he can say that will do an ounce of good, Ethan realizes. Words are not even empty shells in times like these. They are much less than that.

"Well, good luck," Ethan says. "I'm sure you're doing the right thing." As soon as he says this, he regrets it: it is the exact opposite of what he actually believes. He walks over to Chuck, shakes the man's hand, thumps his shoulder, and tells him he'd like to get back to his car now.

"That's fine," Chuck says. Chuck stands there, stiff, holding onto the briefcase. His fingers are clenched around the handle, head bent.

"That snow will melt eventually," Ethan says, turning. "It will."

"Yeah," Chuck says. "I know it."

Ethan walks out of the yard and back down the path. As Ethan walks he realizes he didn't notice Chuck's house. Actually, Ethan didn't know if he could be sure that *was* Chuck's yard. The clouds seem to swell. Suddenly chilled, Ethan pulls his arms to his chest and blows into his hands as he walks past the trunks and branches. Ethan knows the road isn't far off. He bites his lip and walks on.

Furs

"What kind of relationship do we have *anyway*?" Bobby asks. "I mean… There are things—"

Bobby is sitting in the yellow and black striped wing chair. He's sipping seltzer. A wedge of lime bobs on the surface, like a green raft. Bobby notices a brown blotch on the skin of the lime, which dilutes his enjoyment of the seltzer. Bobby has a piercing headache; he wishes he was sitting alone in his office. As much as he complains, he loves his patients—work is soothing. At home he wants to let loose, forget the body. Easier said than done.

"Things, what things?" Janice stands by the window, the spotty shadows from the red maple cascading down on the hardwood. She is tall and thin and attractive. Her calves are muscular, ropey. He should be happy to look at her.

"I'm happy. I am, it's just, you know…"

Janice waits, shakes her head. Her pageboy do jiggles slightly with the movement. They are both off for the day. They decided a month in advance—"couple time," to spend "quality moments" together. Bobby knows these days are fraught with danger—too much time on their hands, the raised level of expectation. Nowhere to go but down.

"Let's get to the brass tacks," Janice says. "What are we going to do?"

"I'm trying to tell you."

"Then tell me."

"I'm trying to, I said."

Janice looks away. She wishes her husband wasn't such a patsy. That's one thing. Sometimes she feels as if she can't breathe. That's another.

"I just feel as if I'm brushed under the rug. My inner needs."

"I, I, I, I," Janice says. "All these I's drive me bonkers, Bobby. Christ, you sound like my therapist. Ex-therapist."

Bobby lifts his glass of seltzer. He immerses his face in his glass. He doesn't think of this as hiding. The wings on the chair help flank him. They also make him feel confined. He remembers when Janice picked the chair. He used to listen to the Sex Pistols and the Clash and now he drinks POM Wonderful and hunts down smoothies and salmon wraps during his lunch break. Things have changed.

"When's the last time? That's all I'm saying." Bobby snorts.

"You make it sound as if it were a colonoscopy, Bobby. 'When's the last time.' Should I schedule doing it on my day planner?"

"Well?"

"I'm not answering that question."

"I don't do it for you any more, do I? I mean, you might value me fine as a person, but it's not the same. Like I was saying, what kind of relationship *do* we have? What is the—"

"It's a *marriage*, Bobby," Janice says, scraping her foot across the floor for emphasis. She immediately thinks of Wilbur. That was the horse's name, right? Bobby still has powdered sugar residue on his upper lip from the donuts. It makes him look childish. Bobby and his idiotic sweets. "It's a married relationship, Bobby. It goes through cycles. We're in a *cycle* right now."

"Like a dishwasher?"

"Maybe."

"Why do you keep repeating my name?"

"Huh?"

"Am I in trouble? What?"

Janice feels a burning inside her. When she closes her eyes at night she imagines a toothed triangle.

"Here's what we're going to do," Janice says. "Like how I didn't use your name that time? Let's get in the car, drive down to Pratt, head down to Pink Flamingoes for a nice lunch—maybe you can get some crab cakes, indulge yourself—then maybe to the BMA afterwards. It will be nice. We haven't seen art in years."

Bobby breathes through his nose, licks his lips. Powdered sugar. He jostles the glass of seltzer, takes a larger gulp. Now the zing of lime is a comfort.

"And after?"

"We'll see."

"We'll see?"

"That's right," Janice says. Bobby grits his teeth, shakes his head.

"You," he says. "Man oh man."

"Me, what?" Janice flashes a half-smile. She thinks she has finally gotten through. So serious.

"You're what they would call a 'high class broad,'" Bobby says. "You know, in the old fifties movies. You trying to *drive* me to do something we'll both regret? Is that the deal?"

Janice shrugs, slips on her red pumps, Bobby stands, downs the rest of the water. Bobby throws on his brown corduroy jacket. It reminds him, somehow, of his twenties. He used to carry a joint in the inner pocket, wrapped in aluminum foil. He doesn't know if it's just his imagination but he still feels as if the jacket carries a faint pot odor. Janice surely wouldn't approve. Bobby thinks of himself as the worst kind of sellout. At the hospital he's known as Nurse Betty. He doesn't mind the term of endearment one bit. Their lives *are* so different.

Janice withdraws her full-length fur coat made of fox pelts, turns around so Bobby can slip it onto her shoulders. He holds the coat with two fingers, at arm's length. Bobby knew his wife owned it, but he'd never seen her actually wear it, much less during the day in the early fall. It's fifty degrees outside, Bobby thinks, what does she need a fur for?

"This is what you're wearing?"

"Sure, let's give it a whirl."

"There are ten fox heads staring at me. It's not cool. It's creepy." He holds the coat, smells it. It smells mostly of musty storage. He can imagine the foxes running about in some pine forest, chasing field mice and rabbits. Next thing you know, wham—they are dead dangling inexplicably on some lady's shoulder. Janice's shoulders are broad and stiff. The string of pearls around her neck. The tanning salon tan. Her expense account.

"I have no idea what I'm doing," he says. "You know that." Janice cranes her neck, glances over her shoulder at him. Bobby can see by the glint in her eyes—she either won't acknowledge the double meaning or doesn't get it. Either way it's bad.

"Put it over my shoulders, Bobby. Let's go." Bobby does, despite himself. He lets the weight of the fur fall. Her shoulders catch it square. That's that. That's that.

Behind Me

I can feel their eyes on me. I don't mind it. The one behind me to the right wears pleated pants, smells of leather and cologne and a whiff of suntan lotion. He's talking about his leagues. Sports, sports, sports: like I care. The other one is the listener. He's glum, smoking a clove to the nub, holding it like a blunt, nodding his dark and glistening hair. He's older. His forehead crinkles, striking worry lines. His eyes are on my shoulder blades, arms, waist. The other goes directly to the more concealed areas. Feeling the invisible brush of eyes: what kind of sixth sense is this?

I'm wearing my black and white shirt, the striped one. Freckling in the sun, I can feel the vitamin D soak into my eyelids. This is life. We're out at the concert, listening to the tender pluck, snap, pluck. The instrumental guitarist brings tears to my eyes. Wishing I could play an instrument. Never had the talent, really. My mother encouraged me, to no avail. Recorder lessons. A bit of piano. Never took.

When I was a little girl, I was a little girl. Did they pay me any mind then? Hell no. But now that I'm gangly and reclining on the grass they'd have me in a second. It doesn't bother me, I swear. It's flattering actually. I mean, it is. If they weren't behind me maybe I'd give one of them a shot. Not both. I'm not... Degraded, immoral stuff. Not that they would mind that one bit, or at least one of them. The other one would hold me tight no matter what. He would love me. The listener.

The guitarist finishes one shimmering, pretty number and the crowd claps. The picnickers swish wine glasses, nibble on cheese, carrot sticks, cherry tomatoes. The sporty cologne man whistles between his teeth. The melancholy clove smoker claps slowly, holding the nub between his teeth. It's almost overwhelming: the smell of grass and mulch and pine needles and clove cigarettes. The guitarist clinks and clanks and picks his way through the next number, tapping his right foot to keep time. One man and a brown guitar. I have to admit, I am jealous of his enthusiasm.

Why am I empty and diffuse?

Then the hushed baritone: "Do you have the time?"

I do, and I tell him without looking back. In the past he could tell by the angle of the sun. All that lost knowledge. My wrists are thicker than I want them to be. Ankles too. The clove smoker looks at my larger-than-normal hands.

"You know," I say, softly, fixing my gaze on the guitarist. I fix a light irony in my voice. "I'm not really a big fan of people looking over my shoulder. They say there is some biological element in that, something about defending against predators."

The guitarist shakes the hair out of his face, lifts his head to the sun. I do the same. That golden orb. My peripheral vision: a thin weed waggling between the smirky teeth of the sporty guy, the seedy end of it dangling, probing the air. I wave a huddle of gnats away.

"What?" the melancholy man says. "I couldn't hear you."

The other one snorts. At least one of them could—the one I wanted to.

"Never mind," I say, shaking my head. "It's not that important."

I watch the clouds scud by, close my eyes, bob my head. In the darkness I can see the clouds. I can see the leaves, the bark. I picture the entire scene—the picnickers, the men, the guitarist, the grass. Opening my eyes I notice what my imagination missed.

Leave me to my delirium, will you?

"You want to dance?" the melancholy man asks me, leaning forward. He doesn't touch me, though I wouldn't mind. I wouldn't mind if he simply brushed his hand across my shoulder blades, accidental or not. I turn to see him. I hadn't noticed the cluster of light freckles on his nose, the way his mouth purses. He has bow-like, full lips, lips a fashion model would kill for—bee-stung. He stubs his clove into the grass, points to the far left of the stage. Men and women sway in the plum shade, under the wavering leaves, sandaled and barefoot men and women arms encircling waists, shoulder blades. I watch them move. They move. I feel something resonate in the lining of my stomach.

"Sure," I say. "Why not?"

He stands, holds out his hand to me, lifts me from the grass. His friend doesn't watch us at all. I don't care. There is little I do care about. We sway, sway, sway.

Upgrade

Halloween

It takes time, but so does everything, Bela thinks. He finds another job—at a warehouse packing educational supplies. The odor of cardboard and foam peanuts doesn't bother him. Bela thinks of the job as an upgrade. The whir of industrial fans. Big Gulp sweating by the tape canister. At night he sends a postcard home, watching reality television on low.

On Halloween the warehouse employees dress up as sheep. The union's idea of a joke on management. Bela goes along. He doesn't mind the feeling of having a tail. That afternoon Bela hears on the local news that one Mara Balogh was found dead on the 4500 block of Pennsylvania Avenue, in a parking lot outside of a liquor store. Stabbed. Drug-related murder, or so the newscaster reports. One of three hundred fifty eight this year alone—though the first Hungarian-American victim this year.

Over one a day, Bela thinks. One a day.

He wants to hit something, destroy something. He holds his temples in both hands. His fingers flutter, bat-like. Bela can imagine Mara's punctured gut. Bela knows he could have done something, anything.

Labor Day

Bela is fired when the entire night's worth of cash just disappears. Bela knows what happened to the money, he just doesn't understand *how* it happened. The booth is never unoccupied—he tends to piss in wide-mouth Gatorade jugs. For the other, there is a Port-o-potty. Bela always locks the booth though—never forgets. Maybe Mara staked him out, made a copy of the keys. This is the only explanation he knows of, though he hopes it isn't true. Mr. Stanley doesn't believe Bela. He hasn't liked him since he began taping photos of Victoria Secret models to the inside of the booth. Bela doesn't understand these prudish American types. The religious. Bela *knows* he is disposable.

Bela calls Mara three, four times a day on his cell. Bela leaves messages. No use. He hasn't spoken to his nephew in months. He can't even assure himself that Mara stole the money. Bela doesn't sleep well. When he closes his eyes his heart races.

Independence Day

Mara wanders the streets—this is what worries Bela. Even though Mara says he *isn't* hooked, Bela can tell. One look at his arms says it all. One look at his ragged, haunted face even. Bela feels as if he is *responsible* for his nephew, even though he only planned on having Mara visit for two weeks. Two weeks became two months. Bela hasn't spoken to Mara in ten, eleven days. Bela asks around but nobody has seen the kid. Writing a postcard to his parents isn't something Bela wants to do, but he considers it. He can't afford a phone call.

Bela doesn't like to leave the booth, but sometimes he can't help it. Sometimes a driver has a question, or a problem. Bela is in the same situation here with Mara. When his shift ends at 5:00 a.m., Bela searches for his nephew. The sky is still streaked by the remnants of the Inner Harbor fireworks. Bela walks in ever-expanding circles, trying to find Mara. He whispers down alleys, behind Dumpsters. Nothing.

May Day

His nephew is visiting and Bela enjoys the company. Even though Bela only rents a single basement room, his nephew doesn't complain once. Mara goes to school in Michigan and says he has met many friends—even has an American girlfriend. Bela is more awed than jealous. "You do what you want when I'm at work," Bela says. He likes Mara, but doesn't exactly have faith in him. Still…

"Yes, yes," Mara says. And he does: he eats fish sticks and oranges and watches television and naps. Bela calls Mara to see how he's doing. "Fine," Mara always says. "Chillin'." Mara smells of smoke and beer.

Bela finds the busy baseball season routine rhythmic. He asks drivers if the Orioles won, even if he already knows. Bela knows, usually, simply by the hour at which people begin returning to their cars. Rhythm. When they are gone, Bela stares at the Shell station across Pratt Street. The lights glow like some alien spacecraft in the dark of the night.

April Fool's Day

This year it is also the first day of the baseball season—Mr. Stanley is correct about the increased parking. When Bela arrives, at 7:00 p.m. the lot is almost full. Charlice shakes her bronzed ringlets. After eight the lot is full and aside from sliding the sawhorses in front of the entrance, Bela can enjoy a break. He drinks orange juice and texts his nephew in Detroit—his only family in the states. He looks at Gisselle, Allesandra, Nikki, Adriana. They beam down upon him, exotic cherubim from another world.

Bela wishes his English were better. He'd like to take classes at the community college, but he can't afford it. He sends a third of his pay to his mother and barely has enough to cover rent, food, bills. He wishes he weren't so big boned, bison-headed, lumbering. He'd like to look across a table at a woman like Adriana. That smile.

St. Patrick's Day

Bela is mystified why a holiday is devoted to some Irish saint. This is America, Bela thinks. Don't they have their own saints? Again, another color. Are all holidays color-coded? Baltimore is a manageable city to Bela. He lives on Paca Street and can walk to the parking lot. His neighbors tell him there have been robberies, murders, but Bela doesn't own anything worth stealing, and he doesn't *know* anyone. Who would kill him? He's *nobody*.

Mr. Stanley told Bela the spring and summer are busy— when the baseball season begins. Even though the Park n' Pay is eight blocks from Camden Yards, it serves as overflow parking. "More people out and about when the weather becomes nice," Mr. Stanley said. Mr. Stanley wears cologne that smells of burnt rosemary.

Valentine's Day

Bela does not understand the purpose of a day devoted to love. Red? Why red? Why not gray or olive-green? Bela doesn't believe love possesses a color. His shift begins at 7:00 p.m. By this time the lot is usually deserted, but tonight it is half-full. He knows tomorrow it will return to normal: four or five cars. Tedium. Bela has the supermodels to help with this. He has these taped to the booth, directly above the external window. Victoria's Secret catalogues are free. Bela is thankful for small favors. Adriana smiles down at him, her breasts pressing forward in a lacy red bra. She smiles like a cat that ate a bird. Bela listens to compact disks from his home country. He only owns three compact disks of Hungarian music though. Sometimes he listens to hip-hop. 2-Pac and Biggie.

Bela collects the money, makes change. A good number of drivers look tipsy. Several couples fight, scowls scarring the night. Bela is comfortable in his booth. Though his job is tedious, he makes much more money than he could in Budapest, not to mention the small towns. Eight dollars an hour is nothing to scoff at.

Backless

--Maybe it's an accident, Lucky says.

--There are no accidents. Sven picks his nose, wipes his finger into Lucky's hair. Lucky punches Sven, kicks his shin. Lucky rubs at his head with the cuff of his flannel, the elbows worn thin. He can see his skin through the thin cotton material. They both hate living in the gray box house with a crosswalk for a front yard, but Lucky hates it more. Sven was cut from the track and field team. His father said he was fast. Not fast enough. Their father works three jobs— dishwasher, car mechanic's assistant, yard work on weekends. Their mother works two—cleaning houses, waitressing. Always working, doing something, always working.

--You know that stupid poem is about Satan, Sven says. The stupid little room to hide in. Don't you see? Sven chucks the book onto the checkered chair. The beige stuffing puffs out of the holes like pus.

--Is not. Like that poem. My favorite one of them.

--It's "Day Star," idiot. Mr. Nelson said in Latin that means Lucifer. What do you think Lucifer means? Mr. Nelson told us.

--Maybe it's an accident.

--Go ahead and cry now, Sven says. You know you want to.

Lucky is cutting the backs out of two three-quarter length

shirts. Their mother picked up a box from Goodwill last week. They don't think about shame. Lucky only thinks about ways to get around doing the things they don't want to do. He considers that one thing in life he's good at.

--There are so accidents, Lucky says. Like names, where you're born, who your parents are, who your numbskull brother is. You don't choose those, Lucky thinks.

Sven pushes his brother from the kitchen table onto the floor. The glass of murky water spills. The chair lands on top of Lucky's leg.

--I guess you're right.

--See.

--Aren't you gonna fight back? Why don't you ever fight back?

Lucky lifts himself from the floor, rights the chair. He pulls the hair out of his face.

--Just shut up, Lucky says. Your stupid yap.

Lucky hands Sven a backless shirt and he puts it on and Lucky puts his on and they turn around and look at each other's backs and they laugh and run around in circles in the kitchen to watch the cheap cotton flail. If Lucky hadn't already sniffed he wouldn't be so into it, but he did. That wasn't an accident, Lucky thinks.

--Where is it? Lucky points to the phone book under the papers and paper bags from Wendy's and Taco Bell. Sven pulls out the glue, takes off the cap, sticks his face into it.

--I feel like I'm getting dumber, Sven says. But I really don't fucking care. I wish I could invent something. I'm too lazy, I know it.

--You're not lazy, Lucky says.

--I'm a lazy fuck, Sven says. What do you think? I don't know a thing. So are you.

Lucky pulls out two more numbered shirts from the cardboard box. Eight and Fifteen. One has yellow sleeves, another has green. Lucky guesses a softball team donated their old jerseys. The kitchen smells. Like rotten eggs. Like sour milk. Like moldering potatoes. Lucky wonders if a mouse died behind the refrigerator again. That would make sense.

He goes up to the roof and plays the spoons. Sven comes up later and watches. The sun goes down just under the electric line.

When their mother comes home it's ten p.m. When their father comes home it's midnight. Lucky is usually in bed by eleven.

This night their mother is wearing a tiara surrounded by sprigs of plastic ivy. They had a May Day celebration at Luke's Grill.

--You look like a demented fairy, Sven says. Lucky snorts.

--I'm a dryad, his mother says, removing the headgear. What did you eat?
Sven shrugs. She points to Lucky.

--How about you?

--Well, let me whip you up something then. You can't just not eat dinner.

--What about you? Sven says.

--I had grilled chicken, as usual. And a salad, thanks for asking.

She puts frozen pot pies in the toaster oven and Lucky sits at the table listening to them sizzle. Sven rests his head in the crook of his arm, casually playing a videogame. Their mother hands them each a cup of apple juice.

--Am I ten? Sven says.

--You don't know how old you are yet? What do they teach

you at school, hon?

Lucky is relieved she is home. He reminds himself not to say a negative thing. She doesn't like the word "hate." She says she wants to live in a safe haven.

When the pot pies are cooked she serves them to Sven and Lucky. They eat and their mother watches them eat. Lucky feels wanted. He sniffs and tells himself he won't ever do another bad thing. The look on Sven's face is blank. His videogame character is bashing a police officer's head in with a baseball bat. Sven's fingers are moving quickly.

When their father finally comes home he flips on the television and Lucky watches him. Lucky fingers the carpet and re-reads "Daystar." He still doesn't see evil in the poem. It's just about a woman and her life, how she needs to find alone time. It is what it is.

Lucky's father looks shorter than he used to. His face is thinner. His skin looks yellow. His stomach is oddly round, as if he swallowed a watermelon whole.

--Hey kid, he says. Lucky watches his father pour himself a vodka tonic and then down it. Then he pours himself another and downs that.

--Didja eat already? Lucky asks.

--Yeah, I ate.

--Whatdja eat?

His father looks at Lucky, *through* him really. Lucky can feel his father's eyes boring into his face, searching for a secret. Lucky's father isn't an angry man, but he can be stern. He can bristle. Sven is asleep on the couch. Lucky's mother is upstairs reading an article about the French Riviera; he can hear her flip the pages of the travel magazine. Lucky can't remember the last time they went on a family vacation. Maybe they never did.

—I ate food, what did you eat?

Lucky knows that's a question he shouldn't answer. His father opens a bag of potato chips and begins to eat them. He doesn't offer any to Lucky.

His father leans back on the recliner, looks at Sven and rubs his forehead. He flips the channels for several minutes, the room changing from green to blue to red to white. His father finally settles on Sportscenter. Lucky closes his schoolbook, stands up. As he walks to his room he pats the back of his father's recliner. The chair bobbles just a bit. Lucky doubts if his father even notices. He realizes he's still wearing his backless shirt. Glancing over his shoulder he glimpses the edge of his naked back. Nobody said a thing about it.

Cranberry Child

My ninety-one-year-old grandmother sat on the floor, opened the grubby, white shoe box in between her legs. She wore one red sock, one ocher sock. The red sock was decorated with white snowflakes. I could smell something like boiled cabbage on her breath. Rooting in the shoebox, my grandmother mumbled to herself.

"I was one," she said, clicking her jaw. Her ring finger taps the box.

One what? I sat, fingered a ball of lint in my jeans pocket and analyzed the small creases in my black leather pumps. I was there for my mother who lived in Kansas City at the time. One what? I thought I had better things to do but every Sunday morning I was there. At the time I was floundering—jobless, no husband, no focus. I was green and immature then, and I was lost. Duty can bring out the best and worst in me.

"Here it is," she said, withdrawing a raggedy photo. The back read 1924. "Here." She handed it to me. "That's me."

I looked at it for a long time. I could feel my breathing slow.

"How old were you?"

"1924. About ten," she said. "Maybe ten."

The photo was remarkable and obscure. My grandmother stood in a swath of sand, barefoot, facing the camera. She wore a black dress with a cloth necklace of some kind and a white kerchief over her head. Underneath her kerchief spilled her black hair, shoots looping as far down as the top of her dress. In front of her was a desiccated stump, and off to the left and in the background were bushes of some sort and a horizontal line of wetness cutting through the landscape. But what I didn't expect to see: in my grandmother's young hands were two large wooden boxes held with string looped around her wrists. I couldn't determine the contents of the boxes, but they looked heavy. The one on her right was marked 580 across the grain. In the photograph my grandmother looked directly into the camera, without shame. There was even a hint of a smile. Her feet pointed off to the stump, as if she was resting.

My grandmother sighed and tapped the tip of her fingernail on the photograph.

"When I was a young girl, I worked. I worked a whole lot." She didn't look at me. My grandmother was sometimes coy.

I knew what she meant here. I understood.

"How long did you do that?"

"Do you know what those are?" I shook my head. "I picked cranberries. You think about this next time you eat Thanksgiving. *All day* I picked cranberries. From early in the morning until the sun was about to set. I did this every year because my parents needed me to do it."

"I see," I said. "You want me to find work, put my nose to the grindstone."

She didn't respond. Instead, she closed the lid, leaned back on the floor, closed her eyes. I could see the little girl still in her—this after the two marriages, the four children, the wear and tear of year after year. She still had the same sly smile. She always must have known something, something others didn't. It was just a passing thought but I wondered then if my grandmother had a long-time lover or has a secret treasure chest hidden in the backyard.

"I was happy to be a cranberry child," she said. "I think I learned a lot there. I was always a daydreamer, and it wasn't much to bend over and pick cranberries while I was thinking and dreaming. It was fine." It wasn't a stretch for me to see the connection. I sat and stared at her for a long time. She looked away, then dug for more photographs to show me.

I'm a dreamer also, I thought, a daydreamer half-wanting my own fair dose of 580.

Status Quo

She has me sit here and watch her. I don't want to. I've never cared one way or another about the way I look. Why should she? I follow the rules of basic hygiene, but that's about all I ask of myself. Of herself she asks quite a bit more.

So I'm sitting in a bumpy wingback chair in Venice on a late July evening. This is the last leg of our trip and I'm ready to return to St. Louis. From the open window I can smell the Grand Canal. I can hear some kind of metallic clanking, which sounds like a quarter against a flagpole. This surprises me, since the air this morning has been almost perfectly still.

I tell Susan she looks beautiful as is. I'm ready to eat, to get this show on the road, but she doesn't look at me. Instead, she clicks her tongue against her teeth. Susan knows she is a perfectionist, but she takes this as a given. In Padua Susan retreated from me, and she hasn't returned. I'm not concerned; I pulled up my stakes weeks ago.

"It's those boys," I say. "Right?" The room is cast in deep, sonorous shadows. The air feels laden. The small, bedside table is fuzzy with shadows. The sandy mushroom-hued wall catches the light from the window, as does the door, which almost burns in the remaining light.

"No, it's not," she says. She knows which Venetians I'm

talking about—the gaggle of adolescents who loiter a block away, glowering at me, and talking to her in a vulgar Italian. Lewd.

She pivots her shoulders toward me, looks over the high point of her left shoulder. It is as if she was driving and needed to change lanes. Her white blouse shows off her figure, and she smooths down her skirt with her hands. She looks at herself like this for a long time. She is angular—thin, pointy nose; high forehead; sharp elbows; bony, veiny hands. Her clasping Cleopatra-esque bracelet looks as if it may fall off her wrist.

The boys believe Susan is Italian, or at least Greek. Susan doesn't speak a word of Italian, though the boys think she is playing hard to get. They called me "fratello," her brother. Susan is *not* my sister, I tried to tell them. I draped my arm around her shoulder and kissed her. I thought this was enough of a signal. They laughed at me—as if this proved anything. In their eyes I was showing off.

Then again, I'm not sure what is left.

"So what do you think?" Susan asks me. She looks at her legs in the mirror, then her eyes rise. "Bill, do I at least look… adequate?"

Why does our conversation have to revolve around her? I. Don't. Care. I want to tell her she looks terrible, that even the loitering boys would turn away from this purposeful exhibition. I want to tell her that her thicket of curly hair looks like a ridiculous clown wig. I want to tell her I'm leaving, going home, never to return, ciao.

"Yes," I say, instead. "It's fine." My voice is flat, and she continues looking over her shoulder at herself in the mirror, oscillating her hips slightly.

This is a story about two people who once loved each other and have since fallen out of love. When we were young my heart would smolder for Susan. I needed her, a physical ache. Now I'm onto bigger, better; I've climbed the ladder perhaps. Susan is right back where we started. For her absolutely nothing has changed. She's status quo. I'm not interested in treading water, maintaining what we already have.

Yet I don't blame her.

I'm staring at the brass doorknob. I'm staring at the reflection of it in the mirror. The picture frame above the bed is cloaked in shadow. I squint to see what the image depicts. It looks like a crumbling edifice to me. Susan tells me it's a famous, historic villa, but I'm not sure I see the difference. The clanking stops, but I can hear seagulls.

"It's time to go," I tell her. She looks at me as if I'm a stranger. Perhaps I already am.

11. ME, ME, ME

A Sunday Story

I'm not sure exactly how or why I lost my way: I just did. For a year I traveled aimlessly, driving from town to town. No real purpose. My wife of nine years left me for another man, and I guess I was trying to right the ship. Believe me, I didn't think of this as a vacation. I avoided tourist spots. This is how I found myself in Chillicothe, Jackson, Point Pleasant, Nitro, Sutton, up through Morgantown, and then into Cumberland.

When I woke up that morning part of my brain thought I was still back in Tulsa, but I left there a week ago. I pealed back my blanket. One thing about sleeping in a pickup is it doesn't take much to clean house and move out. It meant rolling the foam pad, the tarp, and folding the blankets into a tight square that I kept behind the passenger's side seat. On the seat itself I kept a bag of my necessities and usually some bread and fruit and potato chips. That day I didn't have anything in the food bag at all. I was worn to the bone.

As I pulled myself together that morning I could hear the shutter-shutter-shutter sound of a car struggling to start about half a mile away. The back of the brick building facing the parking lot didn't exactly tell me where I was. I thought it was odd that the parking lot was completely empty, even though it was Sunday. I couldn't remember where I was.

It wasn't until I drove two blocks up that I saw a sign for the Cumberland Post Office. I turned onto what looked like a major street, parked in another empty lot, and walked up the hill. I could hear the sound of bells clanging a couple of blocks over. This didn't bother me. I had enough on me to buy a stack of pancakes and a coffee.

But when I walked to the top of the hill I could see this might be a tougher proposition than I had intended. For blocks all of the storefronts were boarded or dark. I walked past a gas station, stepping over weeds and tufts of grass jutting through the sidewalk. Crows picked at the refuse. The wind tumbled yellowed newspapers along the curb. I checked my reflection in the tinted window of an abandoned Cadillac. I hadn't shaved for weeks and my stubble was greenish and mossy. My hair was tangled. My eyes looked more deeply set than I remembered, and my face felt gaunt and bony.

When the rusted Camaro pulled up onto the curb in front of the abandoned drugstore, I picked up the pace. I didn't run—I didn't want to scare them off. But I waved my arms as if I were stranded an abandoned island. I could see a man and a woman in the car. The passenger-side window cranked down and the smoke poured out onto the sidewalk. My stomach was scoured and dry. I felt like a stray dog.

A man with one arm sat behind the wheel. His t-shirt was cut off at the shoulders, and a tattoo of an upside down tree plummeted from his right shoulder to his elbow. The woman in the passenger seat smiled at me. She was missing her two front teeth and some in the back rows as well from what I could see—the ones that weren't brown. Her hair was curled up to the ceiling of the car, and she had her face caked with makeup and mascara. Underneath the layering was a battlefield of zits.

"Yeah?" she said, flicking her cigarette past me.

"You all know of a restaurant in town? Anything decent?"

"Shit no," the woman said. "Nice joke though. There ain't been nothing in town for years. You gotta go back out to the highway for that." Then she turned to the man and he said something I couldn't make out. The woman told him okay, okay in a hushed voice. Then the woman turned back to me.

"We're heading home. Want to grab something with us?"

"That's, uh, that's real nice of you," I said. "But I don't want to intrude or nothing."

"Our pleasure," the woman said. "We like entertaining, shit like that."

This wasn't what I had in mind. I was repelled by their appearance and by the town in general, but the woman seemed straightforward and honest and I appreciated that.

"All right," I said. I figured why not? What did I have to lose?

The woman stepped out of the car and slid her seat forward. Her legs looked heavy and thick. She had a short torso which made her seem out of balance somehow. Asymmetrical. She pointed to the back seat, and I crawled inside their car.

We pulled up to their house five minutes later, and the one armed man cut the engine and shifted the automatic into park.

Their house was in even worse shape than the Camaro. The shingles were falling off, and half the windows looked boarded up. The paint was spotty and chipped.

When the one armed man opened the door the first thing that hit me was the sound of dripping water. Buckets sat all over the floor. To the left in the middle of the room sat a stack of boxes.

Clothes and bags of trash and brooms and rags were scattered here and there, and the air smelled of sour yogurt.

As we walked down the hall the woman introduced herself as Joyce, and the man said he was C.J. I told them I'm Ivan. He raised his hand in acknowledgement injun-style and he pushed the swinging door to the kitchen open. It was greasy and smudged with yellow fuzz.

C.J. plopped himself at the round, white, Formica table. Joyce said she was sorry it was so stuffy in there. Then she opened a window and pulled a bottle of Sunkist out of the refrigerator, and set it on the table in front of C.J. She brought us two paper cups, but C.J. held the bottle with his hand twisted the cap with his teeth. Then he took a swig straight from the bottle.

"Don't be rude, C.J. Jesus!" Joyce said. Then she turned her back to us, lit the oven and cracked eggs into a skillet. I thought C.J. might come back with something, but then Joyce softly said she was sorry, that she didn't mean anything by it. She softened her voice. Everything felt fragile, as if it might shift at any moment. I could hear Joyce sniffle, and her neck seemed to slump.

"It's okay, Joyce," C.J. said, and then the two of us just sat listening to the sizzle of eggs in the skillet.

"Fried eggs," Joyce said, turning around. Her eyes looked heavy and feral.

"Thanks," I said. "I really appreciate it."

C.J. poured me Sunkist into the paper cup and closed his eyes. I could see the strain in his face.

"In case you're wondering," he said, leaning back in his chair. "We're in the middle of calling it quits. Separating."

"Okay," I said. "I'm real sorry to hear that." I felt like an idiot, but I didn't know what else to say.

I waited for Joyce to say something, to argue, to complain or disagree, but she didn't. When my wife and I split it was ugly. I threw things and we yelled at each other for what seemed like months. Then weeks of silence.

Joyce apologized for not having orange juice, but said she always liked Sunkist better anyway. The eggs were sizzling so loudly I could picture the yolks in my mind. She dumped crackers onto a paper plate and dropped them on the table. She flipped the eggs.

"It's true," she said, back to us. "I'm moving. As soon as I can really. We're not happy about it, but that's the way it is. Ten years down the toilet."

I *wanted* to tell her they made it one more year than my wife and I did. That was something. Thin consolation though, I know.

Joyce brought us the eggs on paper plates, handed us plastic forks—and sat down.

"Dig in," she said.

The eggs were runny and a bit underdone to my tastes, but I ate them anyway, scooping up the yolk with the saltines.

"It's this house," C.J. said. "I'm telling you, it's cursed."

Again I expected an argument from Joyce, but she just slouched and nodded. They told me they were the seventh owners of the house. None of the other couples stayed together after living under this roof either, Joyce said. When they moved in they swore they would turn the tide, but that's not how it turned out.

"And here we are," Joyce said.

"You've got to wonder about some things," C.J. said. I was watching the trunk of his tree tattoo curl with the motion of his arm. In the light the tattoo looked smeared and cobalt. "I mean, we tried our best."

I wanted to ask why they were splitting, but didn't want to cause trouble.

"We did," Joyce said. "In the end we're no better than the rest of them. That's the hardest part to accept. We're no better than nobody."

C.J. mentioned drugs, drinking, cheating, money problems— all the demons that my own ex-wife thankfully spared me. "You know," he said. "The same old shit. I'm too weak to be true, I guess." I wasn't sure what that meant, but it didn't sound good.

"Just tell him, wouldja? We don't love each other no more," Joyce said. "Somehow what we had was a limit, some kind of expiration date hit. All the other factors just wore us down." Joyce carried a plastic bag over to the table and, in one motion, swept everything into it except the Sunkist and my paper cup.

"What would you do if you was us?" C.J. asked.

I gulped my orange soda and thought about what I was going to say before I said it. I hadn't had much luck myself so I wasn't the one to talk. In fact, I could see myself in their shoes, frustrated with circumstance.

"I never married. Not yet at least," I lied. I don't know why, but I didn't want to share any part of myself with them. At the moment I was more interested in their truth than my own. "But things the way they are, I don't see how you can pass this house down to anyone. You know?"

"See," C.J. turned to Joyce. "What did I tell you?" Joyce nodded, and waved C.J. on. I wasn't sure what they had planned.

"Ok," he said.

"It wasn't nobody's fault," Joyce said. "He's a son of a bitch, and I'm just a bitch. That's all there is to it. But the air is out of the balloon and it ain't coming back in. It's tough."

"Yeah, we've been through hell," C.J. said. The way he looked at me, I could buy it.

C.J. took another swig of the Sunkist and passed it to Joyce. They didn't look at each other. C.J. bent forward like he had something to say, but then he shook his head. I think I knew what was running through his mind.

"Let me come clean," C.J. said. "We saw your truck early this morning, before you were even awake I guess."

"Okay," I said. This didn't surprise me. I guess I was a sitting duck.

"Just tell him, wouldja?" Joyce said.

"Well, we was wondering… you seem like you don't have much tying you here.   You're not from around here are you?"

"No," I said. Then they told me.

"Yeah, we figured you wasn't either. We want you to do something for us," C.J. said. "It's got to go. We can't sell it in good conscience, can we? I mean, not with everything we've been through. It ain't like nobody's going to miss it."

I asked him what he meant. I thought of my own moldering home.

"You've got to burn it," C.J. said. "If not you, we have to find somebody else."

I didn't know what to say, or think, or do.

"Well, what do you think?" Joyce asked.

I said I wasn't sure. I asked what's in it for me. How were they going to stop me from getting caught? All those nitpicky legal hang-ups. C.J. said he'd pay me a grand right now, and that I could do it tonight when it was dark. Most of their neighbors moved years ago, he said, and there wasn't nobody to see me. They told me all I had to do is light a match in their bedroom and throw it on the piles of gas soaked rags they already had up there. C.J. and Joyce didn't want any of the furniture in the house anyway—too many bad memories linked to all that stuff. They would have their car running at the top of the hill, and all I would have to do was get in their car and they'd go to the movies. They'd blame the whole thing on faulty wiring, collect the insurance money and start over.

I didn't know what to say. On the one hand it felt like a crime, and burning a perfectly good house down didn't sit well with me. On the other, I could see they needed a clean break, and that this might be their only chance.

"It's all right if you don't do it," C.J. said. "It's just somebody's got to do it. It would just make it easier if it was somebody I actually liked. Not some hobo." I stared at the gap where his arm should have been.

"I'll do it," I said. "Okay."

That day I helped C.J. and Joyce load the things they did want into their old green luggage. I did what I was told. We filled the trunk of their Camaro with a bag of clothes, a bag of photographs and records, a bag of knick-knacks—candlesticks, some jewelry, C.J.'s lucky bowling ball, a box of plates and pots and pans that Joyce wanted to hold onto for the sake of posterity. It was a miserable scene.

What sticks out in my mind are all the things that they left— the four-post bed, most of Joyce's clothes, closets filled with exercise equipment and gifts they said they never used anyway. They told me that they would be able to claim all of this stuff when the insurance check came. I didn't know if that was true or not, but it didn't help me. I asked them if anyone would be suspicious when they saw all the stuff they had in the trunk. C.J. said, "Nobody's going to see it.

We're getting a hotel tonight after the movie. We'll keep all the stuff in there. We're having a romantic night out on the town: how could we be involved?" They told me they'd drop me off at my truck before all this. Let me hit the road.

Once we were done packing them up, Joyce splurged on a package of Wonder Bread. They fed me fried turkey sandwiches for dinner—cold cuts heated up with a package of premixed gravy. Joyce offered me a brown banana but I didn't take her up on that. By this time it was dark and a peculiar silence descended over the town. A dog barked in the distance, but otherwise we could have been in the middle of the country somewhere. I just kept telling myself I was doing my good deed for the day. In my mind I convinced myself it wasn't about the money; I was trying to rectify a bad situation.

For dessert Joyce tossed a package of Oreo cookies on the table, and I ate one. It was soft with staleness but the sugar scratched me where I itched.

"Well, we better get started," Joyce said. "Right?"

C.J. pulled out his wallet and placed it on the table to open it. He pulled out a stack of fifties and I counted them: a thousand dollars, just as they promised. Then he pushed a book of matches toward me and told me the house was in my hands now.

C.J. and Joyce showed me where to go, but I watched them walk out the door first. I watched C.J. put his arm around Joyce's shoulders and Joyce lean into him. The screen door clacked behind them, and I heard the Camaro's engine ignite. They still had a common cause, even if it was destruction. I wanted to like them, I really did.

There isn't much to say about the fire itself. I walked up the stairs to the master bedroom. The gasoline-soaked rags were spread all over the bed like a pyromaniac's stuffed animals. Around here it would be at least half an hour before the fire department got to the house, C.J. said.

But as I pulled a match out of the book, for a moment I wondered if C.J. and Joyce were being straight with me. I had the money in my pocket, but I wondered if their car would actually be there. Maybe it was easier to set me up than help me. If they just took off, then where would I be? It would take me an hour to walk back to my truck and get out of town. By then flames would have engorged the house, and the cops would have scoured the area for suspects. I might be the only stranger in town. Then C.J. and Joyce would definitely get their insurance check.

Maybe I was stupid or ignorant or both, but I struck the match anyway, watching the flame grow in between my fingers. By then I was invested in burning the house too. Some large part of myself needed to do it, damn the consequences. I decided if C.J. and Joyce stiffed me, so be it: I would make do. It couldn't get a whole lot worse anyway. If they were there as planned, then I would be fine. How hard would it be to get out of town? They didn't even know my last name. Or anything about me.

When the match hit the bed burst into flames. I stepped out of the room, pressing my hands against the wall and watching the flames lash their bedroom mirror. For a moment I was almost tempted to throw myself down onto that bed—it looked like a quick way to go.

I don't know what finally made me walk down the stairs and out the door. I don't know why I stood there waiting as the house burned around me, but when I walked outside the night was cool and even quieter than it was before. The stars were above me, and the crickets chirped. I walked up the hill like C.J. showed me, two blocks, one step at a time. Under the ratty locust tree the Camaro sat there idling, as promised. Through the rear windshield C.J. and Joyce waved at me to hurry, hurry, hurry. They looked like I did a year ago, as haunted and beaten-down as I've ever seen. They were right: they had been through hell.

Joyce stood out of the car and opened the door for me, and I slid into the backseat just as I did earlier that day. Joyce slammed the car door and C.J. looked around and in the rearview, and he slowly hit the gas, gliding away from their house. Sitting in the back seat, I dropped the book of matches under Joyce's seat and kicked it underneath. For a moment I was their child. For a moment I forgot all about my abandoned truck back in the parking lot back in town. I just watched the darkness, the dilapidated buildings, and the scraggly trees.

"It's hot in here," I said. "Can you roll a window down?" They did, both of them.

What causes a man to do the things he does? I suppose that's one of the grand mysteries, or something close. But it's difficult to ever connect A to B one hundred percent.

After spending the night in a Day's Inn off the highway, I woke up different. My mind felt scoured clean. It was the best sleep I had in months. Even the constant grumble of eighteen-wheelers didn't bother me. I was a hundred miles east and as anonymous as before.

And I still had a wad of cash in my pocket. I walked across the hotel parking lot to the adjacent IHOP and ordered buckwheat pancakes with a side of bacon. Orange juice. Coffee. The joint was packed to the gills with familes, kids. Laughter. Clinking of utensils. Talk.

I sat alone in a booth and poured a wide line of raspberry

syrup over the stack of pancakes and ate them in five minutes, chasing them down with the bacon, then the OJ. I savored my coffee, watching people come and go, watching the sun angle through the clean windows. I breathed in coffee and sausage and eggs and bacon grease.

At that moment I wondered where Joyce and C.J. were. It took everything they had just to drop me off at my truck, wish me well. Their eyes were already distant, beyond, and I could picture them wandering through Morgantown, Sutton, Nitro, Point Pleasant, and the rest. Separate. Searching for what they lost.

As for me, I was satisfied. Hunched over the coffee, I knew right then where I was heading. My bed. My home and the rest.

Pan Asian

"Let's give Mommy a break," my husband says, winking at me. I'm so exhausted I can't see much less smile. He lifts Hailey and bobs her up and down. Jimmy is lurching down the faux-marble steps with Hailey on his shoulder. "Fisheeees, fisheees, fisheeeeeeeeeeeeees," Hailey screeches. Jimmy is a good sport. The room smells of sautéed pork and onions and pineapple and exotic spices. I love my life, but I have to admit sometimes I would trade it all for a sliver of something new. Just for a moment. Yet, I know the cost is high. We both know couples who have gone down that route. It's not pretty.

The puke stain on the crotch of my jeans is mostly unnoticeable—amazing what a splash of water and a tuft of wet naps will do. Sometimes I'm still surprised by how tall Jimmy is. "A husband isn't just another feel-good accessory," I read in some self-help rag. I breathe deeply, suck on my mango margarita. I wish I had a joint. I'm thinking of those weeks in the foothills above Santa Fe. The smell of creosote. The mountains. The robin's egg sky. Eighteen months ago: how much can change in the beat of a butterfly's wing.

"Yes, those are called koi," Jimmy says. Hailey is pointing. Jimmy flashes me a look. He's intent on not speaking baby talk, which he believes retards growth. I'm fine with this, though I don't have the energy to establish and follow theories. Then again, I have more face time.

The busboy refills my water, pouring from the side of the pitcher. I know they do that to avoid ice logjams, but doesn't this defeat the point of the design? I watch the flying saucer-shaped ice hover and clink against the glass. The glass sweats on the cantaloupe-hued tablecloth. The smiling, moon-faced woman at the portico piano croons soft Polynesian tunes. Each floating number sounds like a lullaby.

The middle-aged man sitting next to us is the only lone diner in the restaurant. He spoons green curry onto his rice, hunches over his plate. The bamboo shoots look like small meditation mats. I'm hungry, ready for our spring rolls. The man is short and his long chin is goateed and his somber eyes bear the strain of distress. I can tell he has been through some life-altering event—death, divorce, financial ruin. Who's to say? Aside from Jimmy's grandmother we've been lucky. In particular, *I've* been lucky.

"How's the food?"

He looks up, startled. He dabs his mouth with the corner of his cloth napkin, nods in approval.

"Sorry, didn't mean to disturb you," I say.

"No problem," he says, tracing his finger down the edge of the glass. I don't see a ring. He has long, handsome fingers. His cuticles catch the honey light. I wonder if he wishes he had a wife, a daughter.

"Fisheeees, fisheees," Hailey screeches again. Jimmy bobs her again. Her pigtails bounce and Jimmy ducks beneath the plastic rattan palm bower overhanging the koi pond. For a moment I can only see his shoulders, his back, a flash of his Old Navy rugby shirt. Jimmy and Hailey are cloaked in shadow. I glance at the man's fingernails again, at the veins on his hand, the small patches of dark hair just above his knuckles. I wonder what he'd be like. My imagination is potent, forceful. For a split second I almost feel woozy with fantasy.

Jimmy lurches up the three stairs. He's quicker on the way up than on the way down, as if he could read the strain of my thoughts. He looks at me inquisitively; he must be hungry too. Hailey eyeballs the ceiling, then peers down to the floor, then at the man next to us, then directly at me. Jimmy plops her in the high chair, slides next to me.

"See the fisheeees, mom," Hailey says, softer now. She yawns. "Fisheees."

Then the waiter brings the spring rolls and turns back toward the kitchen. I watch the steam rise from them, lick upwards. I can feel four eyes on me, then six.

I don't mind.

The steam rises furiously, then Jimmy lifts one with his fork, dips it into the peanut sauce. I do the same, watching the steam continue to rise from the end of the spring roll. I bite into it and the vapor dissipates. Soon it will dissolve completely, without a trace.

Hickory Hollow

One morning I get a call from a crackly cell phone with a bad signal. It's some guy laughing and carrying on, playing music in the background. I can hear his buddies in the back seat trying to keep it under wraps. The caller's voice sounds shaky and untrustworthy from the beginning, like he's got ideas stashed away somewhere. Calls me "partner," "buddy," sounds like he's trying to fit in with me, trying to *convince* me of something.

"I know you require a reservation ahead of time," he says. "But I have paying customers in the car with me and we have guns and we're ready to blow some of those birds away, partner." I can hear laughing in the background and loud music with a beat.

Right then and there I should have told them to turn around, said that we were booked indefinitely. Aside from the fact that I usually required forty-eight hours, I just didn't like catering to guys who sidled up to me too strong. Period. But I didn't listen to myself. I told the guy to come on up. Truth is I wanted the dough. It was February. Business was sluggish at best.

When they finally get here an hour and a half later, they immediately pull their guns out, pointing them around at each other, at the sky, whirling and pretend-shooting everything. Then, out bounds this little squirt-dog the size of a barn rat. Its fur is the color of rotten plywood, and right away it starts running around in circles, yipping like a squirrel in heat, pissing all over everything. They say the sucker has a bladder infection. It wasn't even a kissing cousin to a grouse hunting dog, that was for damn sure. First of all, I tell them, the ruffies are bigger than this squirt. Second, even if this yip-yap dog found anything it wasn't about to fetch and retrieve. Probably scared of a gnat.

I read them the riot act, gave them the house rules (including no gun-pointing, no brandishing), telling them they better constrain their yip-yap dog or the grouse won't fly. Well, the owners were worse. It was three guys in their thirties. One guy must weigh three fifty, flabs of neck skin down to his chest like turkey wattles, and he's smoking cigarettes two at a time with a stupid sneer. Then there's this guy with hair greased back like one of those gangsters in *The Godfather*. He's got earrings and bounces and struts with this smirk on his face that says he knows something you don't. The third guy isn't a guy at all, but a lady in a long red form-hugging coat, with a fur collar made of fox or red mink, and a body that just wouldn't stop. The gangster-guy introduced her as his fiancée, but if I had to put money on it I would have guessed she was getting it from all sides without reservation.

"Let's just get going, can we?" the lady in red pleaded. She chirped to her yip-yap dog and asked where the birds are at. I nodded and said as soon as they signed the pertinent release forms and paid the one fifty per for the privilege of shooting my birds. I told them we could walk the quarter mile soon enough. They must've thought the shooting range was right off the highway. They grumbled and mumbled and traded sips from a single bottle of purified water. I thought that was odd was from the get-go.

My wife and I have always lived here. I grew up in this county, two miles down 236. Went to high school up at Freemount, where I met Jan. After working for thirty years at the lumber yard, I settled on a grouse farm. I figured I could cater to the people around who wanted to pay for an easy mark. There's money in that I heard. A man's got to make do up here, take what he can get. That's what I'm doing. Freelancing.

At the time when this happened I had been at it for three or four years. The extra money the grouse let in more than made up for the property taxes, the grocery bills. Jan and I always kept our expenses down. The grouse money was a supplement, that's all. I was never a hunter myself, and I didn't want to sink away any more dough into start-up.

When I got set up I had one pen and I could release ten or twelve birds a day. That was it. After six months I doubled that. I advertised on the Internet. Word spread. I was amazed how many wannabes from the city outskirts were prepared to plunk down two hundred bucks a pop for a chance to kill a bird. A good number went home empty handed but still were happy to pay anyhow. Driving SUVs and drinking their Starbucks, these folks thought the life I lead was more "in tune." They said we were "woodsy." So they came up here to kill some of our animals, make themselves feel better. There are more of them up here on a regular clip than ever before.

Up here we live a good life. We go to the eleven o'clock service. We take walks along the shoulder of route 218. Our neighbors wave to us when they drive by. Sometimes Janice and I drive to the top of Warren's Peak and look down over the valley. I like being able to point to my house, my yard, the horseshoe pit, the patches of mixed wood, the understory in back, perfect for grouse. From up there I can even see cleared pasture that serves as the shooting range. I can see the barn.

But these wanna-bes think everything's perfect up here. They *romanticize*. I try to tell them our biggest enemy is boredom. People turn to drinking. Obesity is a problem. I try to stick to an occasional beer myself, stay off the hard stuff. Even though it was cancer that got my father, I still believe booze was related somehow. My mother still doesn't drink a sip. We visit her every Sunday night without fail. If you don't have a foundation around you things can crumble quick.

Before a release I like to give the ruffled grouse a treat: a clutch of clover mixed with Saskatoon and alder and hawthorn. The ruffies are up and alert late afternoons, so at least I was giving them a fair shake this time. They go crazy for the clover especially, and they coo and hum like they almost like to be penned up just to eat these goodies. From the perspective of the grouse the whole arrangement makes an odd kind of sense: there's not much to eat out in the icy landscape regardless. They might even want to trade safety for warm shelter and food. I'm their prison guard, and maybe their executioner indirectly, but I don't think I imagine the affection. A good number of the ruffies have been here all year. I don't have these guys long enough to name them, but if I knew they would live longer I would. Sometimes I'm tempted to just shut down the operation altogether, just free the ruffies into the brush, or shoot them myself when I get the urge. Which, knowing me, I wouldn't.

By this time I usually had enough birds to release about forty in ten rounds max. This is what the yuppies paid for. Now I didn't closely inspect the guns this crew brought into the equation, but they weren't using six or seven shot, that's for sure. One guy held a 28-gauge shotgun that would have only wounded the grouse had he been able to hit it in the first place. Inhumane. He flopped the gun around like some he was about to rob a bank. I was about to box the guy in the ears. Nothing worse than a guy with poor muzzle control, and this one thought his gun was a toy. The woman was using a little pistol, like she was out of a cowboy movie saloon. The fat guy was shooting with a fancy-schmantzy crossbow. I didn't really care if they used machine guns as long as they paid, and kept from shooting each other. Either way, the chances were about slim to none.

The whole time the three of them were passing around that water bottle like it was the last water on earth. Just then I realized the water was not water. They broke cardinal rule number one—no drinking and shooting. At this point the earringed guy starts calling for more grouse. He says he couldn't believe none of them hit a single one. It wasn't "legit," he said. I told him, tough luck, we're plum out of birds, but he and fatty didn't care for that worldview.

"Why don't you go catch them then?"

Well, I explained, I couldn't likely *catch* the grouse. That's not the way it works. Even though the grouse sat hiding in the trees a few paces off, they weren't going to exactly climb back into my hands ready to sacrifice themselves to a bunch of lug nuts. If they were smart enough to look up and away they would have had a second shot at most of the birds, but they were too busy getting drunk. "If it is so easy to catch them," I said, "we wouldn't need guns. We could just bash them on the head with a rock." They just stared at me.

I know when to shut up and this was time to do so. They didn't probably know I had a gun on my person, but I wasn't about to get into a showdown with three drunks even if they couldn't hit a barn much less anything close to a moving target.

Here's another thing the three didn't know: fifty yards up the slope I had a cell phone taped to the inner nook of an old hickory hollow. Once I had my cage in the pretense of heading out to collect grouse I headed right for the hickory. I could hear them laughing, calling me a "dumb red neck." They were saying I probably molest the birds when nobody was around. They said I pork my sister. This is when I walked up the slope, dialed the numbers. Even they may have heard of 9-1-1 before.

From the backside of that hickory I watched dusk descend. I listened to them bitching and moaning. I waited. Five minutes later I hear the sirens coming up the valley.

My wife said the blue lights from the police cruisers were almost festive that evening. The way they hit the trees, the side of the house, the kitchen walls. I heard the tussle, the cursing, all the garbage those three spewed out of their mouths. Once they were gone, I cleaned up down at the shed. Locked up. By the time I got back home even the tow truck that came to fetch the Ford Bronco had already rolled out.

That evening I tossed the salad and my wife made macaroni and cheese. We clinked glasses, as always, and downed our water and we ate listening to the news on the radio. I'm a lucky man: my wife is a damn good cook and an even better person. I made a fire and we sat and listened to the crackle of it. After supper I even broke open a new box of cigars and let myself rest my foot on the arm of the couch.

I was almost ready to drift off when my wife said, "You look content." I guess I was. I didn't even feel like watching television. I just wanted to bask in the glow. I have a wife who loves me, a house, land to call my own. Peace and quiet. What more could I ask for?

La Isla de Cangrejos

Last year I took my father down to La Isla de Cangrejos to get his mind off my mother. She died months before but he still wasn't sleeping. His shoulders were knotted in tension and he barely ate or spoke.

"I don't know how to take care of myself," he said. "I can't cook. Cleaning? Forget it. I feel helpless without her." His voice was slow, deliberate. He paused between words, searching for the right ones.

My father had always disliked the ocean, but he had never been to an island beach before. I thought it might make a difference. When we walked out onto the white sand, he stood transfixed. Staring out over the horizon, he would listen to my words of encouragement with only a nod. He sat on the yellow and orange striped complimentary hotel blanket, his tennis shoes tied in precise bows, his hands clenching his knees. My father didn't even wear sunglasses.

The hotel would bring us sandwiches on focaccia and roasted potatoes and strawberry smoothies, and my father would eat and drink with disinterest, staring out over the ocean. I had to wipe his mouth for him once. We breathed the warm, ripe air.

"It's so beautiful," he said. "It's gorgeous." Over and over like that. He didn't swim. He never took his shirt off or tanned. His back was rod straight.

Luckily we were only down there for five nights. At the dinner table my father sank into his usual depressive funk. I asked him if he wanted fettuccini or red snapper—he would tell me to choose.

"I don't care," he said.

In our room he closed his eyes and lay on his bed with his arms crossed at his chest. I wasn't sure if he was asleep or awake, but he didn't move. It almost seemed to me as if he were playing the role of a vampire in a grainy black and white film.

I became bored, restless. I tore through my one novel in a day and the closest bookstore was in the Virgin Islands. We had a television, but I didn't want to wake my father. I sat out on the balcony watching the lizards skitter along the walls chasing beetles. I drank vodka and Schnapps from the mini-bar and stared out over the inky horizon, performing a night version of what my father did during the day.

Then the morning. My father didn't shower, didn't change. He woke up at five-thirty with the sole desire to return to the beautiful view. It reminded him of something, he said. He wasn't sure what, but it was good. Even though I finally went to sleep at one, I helped him get settled at the beach. I sat next to him bleary-eyed, or slept, or went swimming in the warm, almost sticky water.

I wanted to ask my father when he would return to himself. My mother wouldn't approve of this brooding, I almost said. But my father had always been able to work out of his own jams. Why not this one?

Our last day of the trip began like the rest. My father stared out over the horizon like usual: his only movement was blinking.

How he never became stiff or cramped was anybody's guess. It was as if he was some hermit in a desert cave.

But as the sun sank toward the horizon, my father stood up.

"I want to swim," he said.

"Dad," I said. "You're wearing pants."

"Do you want to come in with me?" he asked.

I looked around, as if I could find help amongst the honeymooners reclining along the strand.

"Sure," I said. "Why not?"

And with that he struck a beeline for the water. I hadn't seen my father walk that quickly all week. His head erect, eyes directed before him, my father walked into the waves and I watched him. I almost wanted to take his arm, but he would never have let me.

When the water was at waist level, my father stopped. Then he lifted his arm, and pointed with two fingers, his head shaking.

"Dory is behind my eyes," he said. "That's what it is. She sees what I see."

I expected my father to look at me, to gauge my reaction, but he didn't. He stared out into the sunset and then blinked, his eyes closed.

Three weeks after our trip my father stopped speaking. A month later he was diagnosed with Alzheimer's. He died of a stroke a few weeks ago, but I don't think it was the stroke that killed him.

One day when my father and I were sitting on the beach together, the crabs seemed to swarm us. The island has thirty species of crabs, and at least six or seven surrounded our blanket that day—red and black crabs, speckled grey crabs, large unafraid hermit crabs, blue and yellow crabs, black and gold crabs, hunched flat crabs. They clicked and skittered as if they knew, as if they could sense something within my father. I swatted at them with a towel, but my father didn't move, didn't notice. The crabs kept coming though, righting themselves with their claws, and trudging, one by one, in a direct line for carrion.

A Federal Case

Holidays are the worst. And I don't mean just the notables. Some types hate Mondays, going to the dentist, funerals and the like. Sheep. Followers-of-the-expected. Nine-to-fivers. Listeners-of-perky-morning-radio. Me, I'd take a poke in the eye over Columbus Day (today) or Veterans Day or President's Day. Federal holidays mean she's sleeping in, running the hairdryer, clacking on the computer, gabbing to the Brownie Troop leader or some lady from the PTA or someone from the Libertarian Ladies Club or the Book Club. On the cordless. Talking and clomping above me, talking on the cordless.

I can't write a sentence. Actually, I can't even think of writing a sentence. I view each and every sentence I've ever written as fraudulent and filled with multiple glaring fallacies. The thoughts spiral: My career is shot. I'm worthless; I'll never sell another book, publish another screed. I'll sit down in my moldering cave, cloistered away, and tucked safely in my deductible home office, listening to "authentic" jug band music streaming from some obscure radio station in eastern Arkansas. On holidays I sit around and *wait* for something to happen. I wait for my life to assemble in the way it should. I slouch at the computer, pass the time, hold my breath, waiting for Willa to go to work, which won't happen until the holiday is kaput.

Willa raps on the door four brisk times, as she is want to do. I grunt. She enters. For half a second I peer at my wife. She is an attractive woman: I admit that much. Willa has a shapely figure in the classic Jane Mansfield mold. Hips. Bust. Beautiful face. Little circle of dark freckles by her right ear. Dark hair. Dark eyes. Dark mascara. Etcetera.

"Hannah is on the phone," she says, handing me the smudgy cordless. I want to shoo her off, but she stands there, inspecting me. Willa suspects foul play on my part. Not only that, Willa is paranoid Hannah has aspirations to replace her role and function—to boot her out of her own house and home, land her in some nebulous legal morass. Willa smiles a smile that indicates she finds it ballsy of me to speak to my presumed (her presumption) mistress in her presence on blessed Columbus Day, on this day which celebrates the conquest of scores of native people on this continent but which Willa views as a day of national pride, sans irony. Not that I acknowledge her standpoint; I do, however, understand how it operates.

"Hey there, Hannah." This sounds canned even to me.

"I didn't know Willa was home. She must relish her time off."

Hannah makes an effort, so as to not offend Willa. She shouldn't bother. Nothing has happened. Worse, the better Hannah treats my wife the more suspicious Willa becomes.

"Well, it *is* a holiday," I say. I feel selfish.

Willa arches her eyebrows, as if this statement of fact gave her some kind of direct window to my inner being.

In actuality Hannah is in my employ—as my freelance marketing, promotion guru, etc. I would call her my publicist, but this is too limiting. She writes my Amazon reviews. She arranges readings, manages my website, deals with bookstores. We do not have a physical relationship, though of course I have imagined one in some back corner of my mind. But when has imaging hurt? As a footnote, Hannah weights two fifty nine, walks with a noticeable limp, is pocked with zit scars. Last year she had a cyst the size of a kumquat removed from her underarm. She documented the after-effects of her surgery with digital images she uploaded to Facebook, which was a smidge too much. The moment I described this to Willa is the same moment Willa began to think of Hannah as overly familiar. Hannah's cyst invaded our household.

"I'm not just trying to say she's weird, that's all."

"I can see that," she said. Willa splayed her legs on our cherry hardwood, reaching out to touch her toes, chin to knee. When Willa isn't out making six figures in advertising she's exercising—biking, swimming, aerobics, tennis, mixed martial arts.

"You need to get some exercise," she told me once, squeezing my love handles to punctuate the point. "Aside from whatever communing you do with your computer down there."

Typical. But she is essentially indulgent in her own way—I can stay home and ply my craft, no questions asked.

Well, some questions asked. After all, no free lunch. So I've published ten adventure novels through Writers Press International, a POD publisher, a glorified vanity press. I know this. Hannah knows this. Willa knows this. I try to hide the workings of WPI from anyone other than the inner nonjudgmental sanctum. I don't tell them about the upfront fee, or about the uni-color design, or about the bargain basement paper quality.

Willa harbors "concerns." She likes to get on me at breakfast, tell me she's "disappointed I'm not focused with due diligence on the slew of literary agents who might be able to help me. That's what they're there for," she says, quartering an apple, sipping Tropicana. "Have you sent your work to Jake McCain?" She always has an agent tip from someone in her office. "There's a novelist under every log," she likes to say. I'm not sure I enjoy the comparison to millipedes and salamanders. Perhaps it is apt on some level.

The truth we are very close. We read *National Geographic* together. We lounge in candlelit rooms listening to Enya. We like some of the new, less offensive reality television shows. We hold hands. There are other important areas of interest, plenty of them I'm sure.

Still, sometimes I daydream: I am walking alone along a vast, sandy beach, turquoise water licking my feet, palm fronds wafting hither and thither. I kick my feet in the sand, a spray of white cascading in the buttery glow. All the while I forget about writing, about Willa. It's perfect. Then I remember: Columbus Day. Not much else to do other than grin, stare at the lines and dots on the twelve by twelve screen, hope for a salve there. Short of a deux ex machina I don't see another one in sight.

Metro Man

See that map? I have it memorized. See, watch. Hands over my eyes. Now you pick a color. Green? Easy. From the north: Greenbelt. College Park. P.G. Plaza. West Hyattsville. Fort Totten. George Ave. Columbia Heights. U Street. Shaw. See? Pick another. Enough. Okay.

You ever been to the Takoma station? That's a good one. Shops and stores right near by. Walk two blocks and you can get a nice cold drink of iced tea. Last weekend hit New Carrollton and Landover. Walked around there. Not much around those immediate areas though. Lots of parking. Lots of cars. Good if you have a car. Spacious stations. But not much going on. Today I'm going to Silver Spring. Oh, you too? What's it like? Much going on? Yeah, I'm excited. Upgraded, I hear. Have that one, then Forest Glen up to Glenmont and I'm all done.

Then what? Then what? Then it's quicken the cycle. Been doing this all year. A few every weekend. Five or six. In depth. Rather know what I'm seeing than just check it off. Some of them out there just step out onto the platform and say, "I've been there." Not me. Me, have to see what's around in a mile radius. Don't get any funny stares in the city, but in Vienna they look, they stare. West

Falls Church they look. Some people ask me questions. Things. Don't pay them any mind. Just move on. Pretend you're lost. That's my advice. They won't understand.

Next week I take off. Devote more time to this. Because it's important to focus. Plus it works out perfect because the month is a six. My lucky number, see. Then Thursday is the sixth. That will help. Low numbers are always better. Higher numbers mean complications. Complications aren't helpful with this. Got to wear red. And if I see anyone wearing red shoelaces, I have to get off the train. Saw that once and the guy stole my watch. Took it right off my wrist.

You like my shoes? These are my lucky ones. Mesh. Gotta love mesh. Can feel my feet breathing. Inhale. Exhale. Happy feet make a happy me.

Next week I do the whole circuit faster. Idea is speed it up. Just go out to the platform like the others do. Pop out. Walk around the station. Pop back in. Go to each one in a week. Shouldn't be a problem. Spend a day on red. A day on orange. A day on blue. A day on yellow. A day on green. By then I'm worn thin. Takes about ten minutes for each stop. Depends on when. But factor in breakfast. Factor in lunch. Full day, especially if the trains are slow.

Then July even faster. I do all of the stops in one day. Got to start when they start and go until two. To do the circuit you can't dally. No walking around. Just get off the train and catch the next one. All day. I know I'm the best. How? I just know. It's just true. Want to race? I'll race. Race to my home. That'll be one impossible for you to win.

The Drippage

Inserting a thorn into the hard, shell-like skin under my toe is neither difficult nor painful. I simply wedge it, make the "emergency" appointment, slide my feet into my flip-flops and drive the 1.7 miles down to Fairfax Family Practice. When the slightly plump, Guatemalan nurse calls my name, I pretend-limp. The skin is so thick and calloused down there, I can barely feel it.

"How are you doing today, Giles?"

"Oh, could be better. This darn splinter." I try to play folksy, laugh it off.

She shakes her hand sympathetically, squeezes my arm to punctuate her concern. This alone is worth the twenty five dollar co-pay. She's sweet. Even if I don't know her name.

She guides me to the scale, watching the digital reading. One four three. I'm still a toothpick.

She guides me to the examination room, takes my status. Ten minutes later I have the nurse practitioner and the sweet Guatemalan bent over my calloused foot, a light beaming down on me as they extract the thorn with tweezers. It's a sight to behold.

"Darndest thing," I say. "Guess that's the last time I walk out barefoot to get the paper."

The nurse practitioner shakes her head sympathetically,

holding my knobby foot in her hands. She recites the fable of the lion and the mouse: the mouse removes the thorn from the lion's paw and the lion becomes indebted to him indefinitely.

"So are you saying I owe you?"

She laughs knowingly. I get a sense that she has told this story before.

I have an appointment at Fairfax Family Practice at least once a week. "Constipation." "Headaches." "Insomnia." "Muscle strain." Whatever I can dream up. Great place for companionship of the female order. Better than the Haircuttery, the Gap, the coffee shop.

With all the time I've saved from quitting cigarettes I want to immerse myself in television. Married to Denise, I'd smoke a pack a day. Post-Denise it's just a bad reminder. Nothing wrong with letting my brain drift for a few hours a day. *American Idol. Bones. The Unit. Shark.* I can't follow the shows. They blur. The ads circulate throughout, more memorable than the actual programming. I drift asleep in front of the television. Without the television forget it. I need that background buzz.

Living in an efficiency above a used music store is only temporary, I know. Still, I have redecorated—sans my landlord's permission—with technology. Flat screen TV. Refrigerator with e-mail. Sconces that dim automatically. Recessed speakers in the walls. This also helps drown out the hip-hop they blast from ten to eight every day. I don't mind this—in small doses. Everything in my place buzzes and rattles. Even when they close up shop and turn off the tuneage my apartment still hums, as if a vacuum cleaner rests underneath. Denise lives in our old four bedroom overlooking the lake.

A common but unfair view of divorce is that 1. The ex-husband is to blame. 2. Because he—most likely—cheated. In my case—not to cast aspersions—Denise was bored. As she liked to put it, she "lost respect" for me. It "wasn't one thing." It was "just who I am." Still, I suspect she found Miles long before Denise kicked me out. Just a theory.

Factors for her loss of respect:

--I teach elementary school art, which she views as wussy and unbecoming.

--I like fishing, which she views as hick.

--I went through a bi-curious phase in college, which she can't understand.

--She thinks I'm overly "clingy."

--She made twice as much money as I did and still do. Sue me: I like having my summers off. I also like kids.

As a wussy, clingy, gay hick I didn't have a chance with Denise. I should've married my college girlfriend, Tina, who obsessively painted watercolors of road kill. She was different.

"Hiya," she says. "She" being the woman with the dyed-red, reverse Mohawk, standing next to the stairwell leading from my apartment. She's leaning against the beige siding, chewing gum. I don't see any noticeable nose-rings or piercings or tattoos or various "indie" paraphernalia.

"Hiya," I parrot. "You shop here?"

"Oh, sure," she says. "Just got a cd for my nephew. He's thirteen and I'm trying to introduce him to the Ramones. Figure that's a good start."

"It is," I lie. I've always been partial to The Pretenders or even better, Tchaikovsky.

"What's back there?" she asks, pointing down the grubby corridor to the stairwell.

"Me," I say. "I sleep there."

"Oh," she says.

"Yeah," I say. "That about sums it up for me, also. 'Oh'."

"Does the store annoy you?" I think about *how* I want to respond to this question before I do. She strikes me as possessing a healthy sense of irony and self-mockery, so I decide to be honest.

"I hate it," I say. I don't mention the annoying clusters of teenagers, the poseurs in Dungeons and Dragons garb, the hipper than thou twenty-one-year-olds who dismiss any technical musical question as "pointless."

"Yeah," she says. "That makes sense."

"Okay," I say. "Good."

I tell her it's nice to meet her. She parrots *me* this time. Not bad, I think.

Moving on isn't the easiest thing in the world, I think. I'm driving back home from school. It's a week after the bottle-red redhead and I exchanged ironic pleasantries. It's four-thirty and I have a headache—one of those nagging headaches that doesn't dissipate. Earlier in the day I tried Advil, coffee, a "warm compress," deep breathing. Nothing. I just wanted to bury my head in the sweat-stained pillow on the mattress on my mottled brown industrial carpeting, surrounded by my technology.

When I park and lug myself down the sidewalk towards home I see the redhead again. "Maroonhead" is more apt, actually.

"Hiya," she says.

"Holding the wall up?" I ask.

"Yes, I am. I was worried all that bass might be tearing at the structure."

I'm in a rotten mood, and I don't feel like chitchat. I know I should be polite, advance my relationship with her, if I can. My therapist told me every week to "face my fears." That was four years ago. Now Miles and Denise have two children. What do *I* have?

"Hey, look," I say. "I have a splitting headache and just want to die right now. But if I can lie down for a bit I'd love to chat with you more. I'm bored to death up here. Why don't you come up and you can watch me suffocate myself with my grimy pillow. Or we can have a beer. If you're not busy, I mean."

"Sure," she says. "Why not? I'm Marie."

"Hi, Marie," I say.

I'm submerged in my pillow, a fan oscillating on my face—back-legs-legs-back-face. Two Advil in my bloodstream. I close my eyes. I can hear Marie shuffling around my apartment. This might be disturbing, but for some reason it isn't. I'm so comforted just having her there, fiddling around. I don't process how odd it must seem to her. She closes the blinds, lights a candle.

"You can put some music on if you'd like something soft, mellow."

"Biofeedback?"

"Exactly," I say. Something odd about that word, I think: sounds so cold and calculated. She navigates the I-pod, finds some Paul Desmond. Perfect. As I lie there in pain, she waters my single plant—a dry jade.

She dusts my windowsill and table with my Marti Gras-hued napkins, then sits at the table and crosses her hands, closes her eyes. There is something touching about this.

Half an hour later my headache lifts and I sit up. Marie opens her eyes and looks at me.

"You know," I say. "After my divorce, my eyes turned grey. Isn't that odd?"

"What color were they before?"

"Bluish-hazel, but definitely closer to blue."

"That is very odd," she says.

"Yeah, disturbingly odd. I went to the eye doctor and he said he'd never heard of eyes changing colors in adults, short of contact lenses."

I tell her my theory how and why it happened—stress, stomach acidity, blah, blah. I've practically memorized this speech. My voice sounds pedantic to me suddenly, as if I think I invented the wheel. As if I'm the only one in the world who has thought about eyeball pigmentation.

"Hmmmm," she says.

What else can she say? I feel like a pedantic, hectoring old man.

We decide to order pizza. Not the most original culinary choice, but something I usually don't do—too much cheese, too cheap.

As we eat on the floor, Marie tells me she's a baker, that she walks to work every morning at four thirty. She's done by two in the afternoon. I ask her about her work.

"I do love pressing my hands in the dough," she says. "I love making something that people want. I need to feel needed."

"That must be a good feeling," I say.

"Yeah," she says. "Bread helps."

I fold the tip of a piece into my mouth, asking Marie what else she does. She tells me she's an obsessive cleaner. Her townhouse must always be spotless. She says she cleans two hours a day. She has certain "routines," she says.

"Medication helps," she says. "I love my little pink happy pills."

An OCD Goth who bakes. Excellent.

We polish off all but two slices of the pizza and call it quits. We lean against my loveseat for support. Marie stands up and opens the blinds.

"Let's see those eyes," she says, then bends in front of me and stares.

"They're grey, right?"

"Yeah, grey. That's right. I'll be."

She kisses my forehead and says she'll give me a call.

"You're good people," she says.

I write my phone number on a subscription insert from *The Arts* magazine. She folds it methodically into a small rectangle, glides it into her pocket. That's that, I think.

When Marie does call a few days later it's seven thirty in the morning on a Sunday. She wakes me with the call, immediately apologizing.

"Oh, jeez," she says. "I forgot how early it must be for you."

I can hear a mechanical whirring in the background.

"How's your head?"

"Still present," I say. Confront your fears, I think. I sit up, kick off the sheets.

"That's good," she says.

"You know," I say. "Do you like fish?"

"The animal? The food? The card game? The Deadheady band?"

"As in fishing," I say.

"Oh," she says. "Sure. A nature outing."

So we go. It's not much of a nature outing, per se, in that we drive ten minutes away to a small bridge overlooking a creek which runs down into the Potomac. I've had good luck there before and even if we strike out, it's shady and arboreal.

It's also, unfortunately, drizzly and foggy and as humid as a greenhouse. My t-shirt clings to me. Marie's hair frizzes out. Still, she doesn't complain once, not even when I jab the hook through the worm and wipe the residue on the ass of my jeans. She doesn't complain even though the creek smells of sewage.

We dangle our lines off the bridge for an hour. Nothing. Luckily the tree canopy protects us from most of the drippage. I watch. There is something to this, I think. I can see ripples, movement beneath the surface, but no bites. I'm moved by Marie's stoicism in the face of piss-poor conditions.

"Tell me if this has ever happened to you," I say. She holds her rod loosely, the tip of it paralleling the bridge. We are sitting, our legs dangling between the rails. "You are in the middle of a 'moment.' You know it as you live it. And as you live this moment you are already saddened by the fact that it will end, that pretty soon it will be a memory."

"Yes," she says.

"That's now," I say. I watch the lines by her eyes. I feel her fingers clutch at the fabric of my jeans. I listen to the sound of water dripping. When I close my eyes it's blue.

A Fine Line

1. The invite is wedged between an advertisement from Jiffy Lube and a bill from the gas company. "Come celebrate my official retirement!" This is from my landlord, stamped on a plain white insert. There are directions, a postcard to RSVP. The party is about 45 minutes away. It's definitely unpretentious.

I don't enjoy parties, especially parties with an official occasion. At least I used to. Wilton is a good man. He has bone cancer (in remission), yet he never once raised the rent on me. He worked as a civil servant for forty years. FDA. I still don't particularly want to attend his party, but I know I should.

We do too many things we *must* do.

Yet, sometimes we don't do enough.

I open a can of tuna fish and plop it in a cereal bowl. I sprinkle it with salt and pepper and squirt mustard into the bowl. I stir it with a knife and spread it on toast. That and a Granny Smith apple and a glass of water—dinner.

I prop the invite against the wall in my "breakfast nook," which also serves as my lunch and dinner nook. I inspect it for fissures as I eat.

2. My watch always reads 3:17. It's a good reminder—of what I'm

not sure. I take photographs of myself to mark the time. This is a more direct measure. Every Friday at 3:17 in the same place. Directly outside my front door. I have twelve books of photos filled with these. I believe I look older than I am. I have yet to receive confirmation.

I also take photographs of statues. I have seven photo albums filled with these.

3. I have three jobs, have always enjoyed the diversity. Never understood why someone would work one job when they could allow themselves a broader array of what life has to offer.

It does become difficult when I sell shoes at Penny Feet in the morning, work a lunchtime shift at Thyme Square, and then shelve books at the library at night. On days such as this the boundary blurs between pumps, omelets, and books-on-tape. These complications are few and far between, however.

"Success" is a sucker's deal. I'd rather be a dishwasher than a CEO. Honestly.

4. Jillian calls. Jillian is my new "ex-girlfriend," though this phrase isn't apt. Not only didn't we consummate our relationship, she never so much as saw me naked. I saw her naked many times. So, it didn't work out—this after a year plus. She wants to "stay in touch."

"Why is it that on the days when I don't need to reach you I reach you?"

"I don't know," I say.

"Is this your *actual* voice?"

"Yes," I say.

Jillian once accused me of being robotic and asexual.

"How about lunch? Or are you too busy to eat these days?"

"I can eat," I say. "If you're hungry, I can eat."

"But are *you* hungry?"

"I can take it or leave it."

She tells me I better not stand her up this time. I didn't. I just forgot. Jillian took this as a sign of my "disinterest." She shouldn't take my indifference personally. I'm not easily aroused.

"Tomorrow then?"

"Tomorrow."

5. I blame my undergraduate education: I see myself as some dazed character from a Sartre novel, maybe *Nausea*. When I lift a knife I do think I could stab myself in the eye if I wanted to. When I put oil in my hatchback I imagine possibly drinking it. A fine line exists between stability and the loss of it.

6. Going to a party is not a bad idea—I haven't been to one in years. Co-mingling with my fellow man and all that. It will be nice. For a moment I feel honored to be included.

I can be optimistic if given half a chance.

7. I had a best friend growing up. Ryan. We did everything together, called each other each night, shared secrets. We had a friendship where we would make each other birthday cards crafted with photos from magazines. Craft projects: scissors, glue sticks, sharpies. We memorized mythology pantheons. I was particularly fascinated by the Norse Gods. Loki and Ullr were my favorites. In childhood connection is a kind of currency. In adulthood I'm not sure what, if anything, it means.

I haven't seen him for six years. We spoke (awkwardly) on the phone a year ago. Last I heard he worked as a mortgage broker in Cincinnati. I've thought about calling him many times, but my reservations always stop me. Our falling out was quick and painful.

My closest friend now is a fifteen-year-old boy, Neil, who walks with a severe limp—car accident. He shelves books with me at the Rappahannock Central Library. Sometimes I drive him home. His parents don't wave to me, and they don't look me in the eyes.

8. After I eat I decide to call Ryan. I justify it like this: I'd rather speak to him (even if it's awkward) than Jillian, and I had already committed to *her*.

I get his voice mail.

"This is 571-354-0672. I'm off paying the bills. Leave a message. Call you back as soon as I can."

"Ryan. Keith. Money is far over-rated, Ryan. Call me back to find out why." I leave my number.

9. As I recline on the couch, I read *Intellectuals*, which is more a screed than a book. I feel deceived by the title—I want to chuck it into the trash. I cradle the phone, but it doesn't ring.

As I read I can hear the family below me eat dinner—silverware, ice in glasses, laughter, conversation.

My father calls me "aimless," though my mother calls me "searching." They divorced in '97. Why they couldn't work it out I have no idea.

10. Lunch. The sandwich joint across from Thyme Square. Why Jillian likes this place is beyond me. They specialize in cholesterol injections (the name is deceiving). She orders a steak n' cheese. I order egg salad. We snack on the barbecue chips they "make" in-house. Scrappy's does have a pickle bar though, which is at least

quirky.

Jillian wants to talk about herself—climbing the career ladder, her yoga class, the growth she has noticed in her own ability to relax, her burgeoning retirement account.

"People are so foolish…with their choices," she says. Jillian is in "personal management." I don't understand it.

"Yeah?"

"Yeah. Take this one guy yesterday. Call him 'Dale,' because everything is confidential, you know. Doctor, psychologist, lawyer, personal manager. Same deal."

"Okay," I say. I bite into a sweet pickle.

"He decides to rotate money from his IRA into his checking account, pay the penalty. And why? To go to Barbados for a week. He has zero savings. Goes down there, gets drunk, steps on glass and ends up severing nerves in his feet. Can you believe that? Something symbolic there," she says.

We sit and eat our sandwiches. I watch the ceiling fan.

"When's the last time you had sex, Will? You're smart, handsome. When?"

"A couple years ago."

"A couple years ago?"

"Yeah."

"Want to update your resume?"

"It's not work," I say.

11. A party, huh? I don't know. Maybe it's not such a good idea. Jillian makes me feel as if I'm a social leper. Of course this can be a self-fulfilling prophecy. I should go, I tell myself. I really should.

12. I've never been to therapy. It's not that the idea of it leaves a bad taste in my mouth—though it does. It's not the money—though it *is*

too expensive. Therapy simply entails too much introspection and navel-gazing—it does. I don't want to become one of these characters from some Woody Allen movie, navel-gazing all day long. I'd rather drink oil. Or simply plod through—sell shoes, bus tables.

When I see Neil at the library he listens to my complaints. That's enough.

I also listen to his.

I bring my latest photo album to work.

"Do I look old?" I ask him, during break.

He examines the photos closely, flipping the book.

"They're all the same," he says. "Just light variations, that's all."

"Do I look old?"

"No…but older than you should," he says.

"It's not vanity," I say. "I'm just curious."

13. The to-do list is the hydra of modern society. As soon as one is completed another crops up in its place. Unstoppable.

14. Ryan still hasn't returned my call. It could be he is on vacation, or ill, or hasn't paid his phone bill. All doubtful. More likely: he has zero vested interest.

I hastily examine Wilton's party invite. I check "yes," seal the envelope, send it off.

15. When the day of the party arrives…I can't. Can't bring myself to attend. Though I feel duty impels me—especially because I RSVPed yes—my body vetoes my decision. I know I should call Wilton, at least—offer a white lie (cold, aunt's funeral, and fill in the blank). But I don't. I fail to even perform that common courtesy.

I feel a twinge of guilt, but after a couple glasses of Chianti it dissipates. I recline on the couch staring at the ceiling. I put on some Iggy Pop and turn it up to block out the self-doubt. I feel just fine, for the moment.

16. I half-expect Wilton to call, scolding me. But he doesn't. I half expect a notice from Wilton stating that he's raising my rent. That doesn't happen either. This is the way it goes for me: I cynically expect the worse, but others are much less corroded than I am. As a result, it usually turns out better than I think it will.

Still, I suppose you could say I disappoint myself. Welcome to my world.

I Hear You

I do. I hear you, I hear you.

You're sitting there on my couch because I want you sitting there on my couch. Funny thing, that. Usually in life if/when I want something I get it. You? Not so much. You're off in la-la land, poking an eighteen year old—while married, no less. While married. Do I need to repeat that again?

I've determined if I'm not married by forty I'm marrying myself. I'll give myself a ring, go to the JOP, whisk myself on a honeymoon—somewhere sticky, tropical. It will be magic. I don't care.

No. I don't factor in. I wasn't *asking*. It's not a question.

I find it very interesting—this whole male visual thing. Don't you? Now I am asking. (Yes, you're allowed to nod. Sit there and nod—that's your job. Nodding. Nod away). This whole male obsession with the perfect ass, the perfect set of tits, the perfect stomach. It's not even a question of us—of women—I'm more concerned with *your* well-being. There is something so Vasca Da Gama about the obsessions. If you find the perfect ass-tits-stomach-legs-face-blah-etcetera-blah-blah, then what? What then? What's new becomes old. What's perfect becomes imperfect. You get restless. So what's the point of seeking perfection in the first place?

As for you in particular…since that's our concern here, we both agree. Yes, nod. Good. I know my butt is too large for you. You don't have to say a thing. It doesn't matter. It's my butt. Mine. But I'm the nicest person you'll ever wanna meet. Yes, I have a larger than normal ass. I'll trade that in any day for one hundred and fifty seven friends. These aren't Facebook buddies trading links. I mean, regular friends that I call and speak to, who visit me, who go to the movies with me. One hundred and fifty seven is nothing to scoff at. So my ass may be big, but it has a winning personality. See? And it's mine, not yours. Mine. Mine.

Speaking of personality—what were you thinking drawing me to yours? You know you can be very sweet and considerate. You *trapped* me. No, I'm not saying Venus flytrap. That's histrionic, don't you think? More like quicksand. A slow demise. You sat there at the Lebanese Taverna, plied me with fine olives and hummus. Unfair: you *knew* my weaknesses.

I didn't go to bed with you, that's right. Who in their right mind *would* with your track record? Not only am I not a sperm depository, but I'm a woman who celebrates Pi Day. Could you honesty maintain it down there as I recount digits? I would.

Yeah, take it off. You can remove the Bluetooth from your ear, thanks.

No, I won't. You no longer have a name to me. Your children will be beautiful, I'm sure. The thing is they won't be mine. Ever. What's the cause for celebration? So you have a child. Whoopee. That is what humans are biologically determined to *do*. So is taking a shit. So you can be a human being, congratulations.

What's the difference? Me? Never. I'd end up as one of those women so morose from post-partum depression you'd find me dicing up my own placenta into a marinara sauce. Yeah, that exists.

And you? Your stories. More than anyone else I know you are the sum of your fictions. I find it interesting that you'll tell me all this... this dross. Yet, when it comes time to step up to the plate for some honest-to-goodness self-expression of the "I love you variety," you know what? You're as mum as a porcelain doll.

That's right. I *am* all of those things and more. I'm self-absorbed. I'm a good person trapped in a terrible personality. I can't help myself.

You know why. You know. You're sitting here because I'm not *in love* with my problems. Because you get to lug around these rocks. And yes I know I said I want to be a septic worker. They're the only honest blokes out there. That doesn't mean I'm going to do it. That's right; I'm stealing a page from your book on saying versus doing. Yeah, I find that very interesting. Very much so.

Be my guest. You drink as much of my shitty tap water as you deem fit. You know how much a glass of that costs? Half a cent. Maybe less. You sit there and drink my half a penny of water. It's on me. You know what I'm going to do? I'm going to pull on some sweats, feel sorry for myself. I'm going to listen to the "miserable" Stephen Patrick Morrissey croon and think of the utter *joy* we could have shared together—the dinners, the laughing, the sex, the parties, the snuggling-on-Sunday mornings-while-drinking-cappichinos-and-reading-the-Outlook-Section. Yeah, music expresses my inner feelings for me—if I don't. And sometimes I don't, in all honesty.

Yes, that's the Bible. Get your grubby mitts off—don't you contaminate it. And tuck that smirk back where it belongs. I said you could drink my water, I never said you could paw at my holy book. Yeah, I read it. I read it every day. I may look like I'm the lost daughter of Joni Mitchell, but there's more to me than incense and patchouli.

You know what else is interesting? So I've lost all this weight now. Hip-hip-hurray. Party for Natalie. But the thing of it is, when people call attention to that—when they say, "Natalie, you look so good, so healthy, so pretty, so thin"—I think what, you didn't like me before? Now, I'm "improved"? Does that mean our previous relationship was a fraud? I'm suspicious of compliments.

Don't you see? It's a trap. If you love me and affirm this, I don't believe you. If you don't, sit across from me on my thrift store couch drinking tepid water, listening to me berate you for what you haven't given me (which I wouldn't accept anyway, really).

I'm going for a walk. Yeah, we can look at the maple leaves turning red—all that autumn bullshit. Pumpkins and apple picking and bullshit. Personally, one thing nobody speaks to are the leaf stains on the sidewalk. Nobody talks about cold autumn rain, but it's there all along. It's waiting to come along all the time.

Night Teaching

I admit my flaws.

I never said I'm admirable. And I always knew I'd end up with my just desserts at some point.

I told her there's nothing wrong with night-teaching at a community college. My mother worried I was becoming some kind of pedagogical vampire. I tried to tell her when the sun sets the good students rise. During the day they work as secretaries and computer programmers and then limp their way through my classes with heavy lids and weary minds. They are older and know their priorities. And they pay for their own credits, so they have an incentive. They care.

After class sometimes my students and I will go out drinking. Weekdays the Rusty Oar on Old Mayne Road has two dollar drafts. Wednesdays, drafts are a buck: "Hump Day Special" they call it. I don't know why the Rusty Oar is named the Rusty Oar: there isn't a drop of water around here larger than a puddle or a backyard pond, and oars aren't made of metal anyway.

Every semester I end up sleeping with one of my students, sometimes two if I'm lucky. It's sketchy and unethical as hell, I know, but somehow I can get away with it—I'm still young enough myself, perhaps. I'm not admirable. If the beautiful ones are taken or disinterested I move onto the second tier. If the second tier is taken I move onto the third tier, and so on. My selection process begins and ends with a simple question: do you have children? The answer is usually, "Me? Children? Are you kidding me? I'm not even married. I'm nineteen. I have a boyfriend, but...I'm only..." Fill in the blank.

My target pool? The women who can clearly answer this question in such a way as to indicate they are not involved with anyone at all. Otherwise it gets too messy. By the roster I mark an X next to each woman who is taken, and I draw a smiley face next to the open possibilities. When I began, I assumed beauty and brains go together. Now I know better. I don't think I let it affect my grading system, but I have to admit my female students usually do receive A's.

On the first day of the spring semester one year, I glanced up from the lectern to see Nikki Levering sitting pert, brunette, and nose-ringed front and center. She crisscrossed her legs and plucked her multiple ear piercings. I knew right then. By the second week six or seven of us were downing drafts at The Rusty Oar regularly and I was nudging Nikki and flirting and buying her margaritas on the sly. By week four Nikki was pleasuring me in the backseat of her Dodge Viper. By week six I was eating fried egg sandwiches in her apartment for breakfast, wrapping myself in her stolen plush maroon Hyatt bathrobe.

Then I found out that Nikki had a baby. Not only had I failed to ask Nikki my most basic question, but having already gotten down her pants, it was too late to do the basic screening.

I squeezed my fist into a knot. "What do you mean, kid? Where has the baby been all these weeks?" I hadn't seen any baby paraphernalia, any baby pictures, but Nikki explained that all the rattles and booties are with the baby. I thought this begged some basic explanation.

"The baby's father gets the baby every other day. Since my husband Sean lives two blocks away the judge thought—"

"Husband. What husband?" I said. "What husband? Did you say husband?"

"Yeah, and ever since the separation the baby's our little hot potato. It's not a problem is it?"

"No, it's not," I said. "Not at all. No. *What the hell?*"

"Like I said, we're separated."

"I knew absolutely *none* of this."

But when I opened the front door to Nikki's apartment the next week, the baby was squalling in his living room crib, face red, arms smashing the mattress, feet treading invisible water. We were tipsy already, and we had eaten some great fajitas that night. I dropped the six-pack on the floor and covered my ears. In my life I had never heard such a piercing cry: like a car alarm, but five times worse.

"Aren't you going to do anything here?" I asked. "What is its problem?"

"*He.* Not 'it.' He's okay," she said. "If he shat his pants it ain't going nowhere, is it?" She had a nice smile. Dimples. Love those.

"Maybe it's hungry. Did you leave him here during class?"

"Yeah," she said. "But it's fine. He can't go anywhere on his own, can he?"

I didn't know what to say to that. I guess she was technically right. Then Nikki picked up the baby. For a mere moment the baby hushed and I lifted my hands from my ears. But then Nikki placed the baby on the kitchen floor, where it started rocking back and forth on his back like a beetle.

"Why don't we go have some fun?" Nikki said, lowering her

head and pointing to the bedroom. She zapped the TV on and turned the volume up full-blast. Then she closed the door. The sex was usually good, I suppose, but this time the screaming baby and the blasting infomercial about the ultimate wet-dry vac took something away from the mood.

"Can't you do anything about the crying?" I asked as I entered her.

"No," she said. "He's always like that when I have a guy over. He's showing he disapproves or something. I bet the little sucker will grow up to be the lead singer for some heavy metal group."

In thirty seconds I wilted.

"Shut that thing up, Nikki," I said. "Please. Or I will."

"Will you now?" she said, pushing me off her.

"Yeah," I said.

"What are you going to do, lecture to him about the Spanish-American war? What, you going to bore him to death with the Alamo, or something?"

When I plodded out to the kitchen the baby was crying so hard I thought he might burst into a thousand pieces right there on the linoleum. I scooped the sucker up and held him to my breast, as if I could nurse him. I expected the baby to keep screeching and perhaps upchuck on my polo shirt. Instead, he actually stopped crying almost immediately and then he looked up at me. The baby's skin was as red as a clown's nose, and he smelled like diarrhea, but the moment I picked him up something happened. There I was, a forty one year old history professor holding a baby boy in my twenty-something student's house. It was odd and pathetic at the same time, and somehow *human*. I hadn't felt that way in years.

Naked and limp I turned off the television and carried the baby through the doorway to his mother. The dark bedroom was cool and pleasant and for a moment I imagined we were in some dank primordial cave from some early tribe of humans. I held the little guy tighter and sat on the bed next to Nikki. With the baby cooing and gurgling, I let Nikki do her thing, and she did it, and did it well. I had to look away.

By the end of the semester Nikki had dropped the course. She stopped attending class, didn't answer her phone. That summer she called me out of the blue and told me that her husband came back and that her baby was crawling and could almost stand. She also told me this was it: she wouldn't talk to me again. She just wanted to let me know what happened to her. Sorry, but I was a mistake, she said. Her husband was in the other room, she whispered.

"Anything you want to say to me?" I was irate.

"I have to go."

"I have something to ask you," I said.

"Yeah? Make it quick."

"Does the baby still scream?" I asked. The pause was heavy.

"Hardly at all anymore," Nikki said. "I guess we're lucky that way." Then she hung up on me.

Wire

No, I'm glad you called. Listen. He's not here, and I don't know where he is, to tell you the truth. I haven't known where he is for years really. No, it's okay. It's okay. I guess he called two years back, or close to it. Back then he was living in New Mexico somewhere, I'm sure. No, not Taos—nowhere you've heard of. Nothing on the radar. Look, even if I knew, I had no way of contacting him. No address. No phone number. Not even a town. If I had a town I could call the station to see if they knew anything, but I didn't, so it was my tough luck, and it still is.

Now you might think I'm unconcerned, but I'm not. When was the last time you spoke with him? That long ago? Well, then I might actually know *more* than you do, believe it or not. That would be a first.

Four years ago I woke up at my usual time. Seven o'clock. Walked out to pick up the paper, check the stocks, the box scores. I looked up from my slippers, and where my Range Rover should've been there's a slab of concrete. Nothing. That's right. Yeah. You guessed it.

No, I didn't bother to call them. I just assumed it was his. If he wanted to cut me out—cut *us* out—it was his. Fine.

Two weeks later I got the call. He was in Raleigh, North Carolina. Two weeks and he only made it one state down. Isn't that pitiful? He was shacked up with some filthy, grungy, hippie-assholes in the shabby part of town. A crack house. A heroin house, whatever you want to call it. My skin crawls just thinking about it.

No, I know. He wasn't into any of that back in those days, you know. He was a good kid. It's not your fault. What could you do?

He had sold the Rover for two grand. *Blue Book* it was worth at least six at that point, and that was with a ton of miles on it. Why? He had that poison in him. He just had to have more, you know, you know, you know. He only cared about that electric *feeling*.

Right. He was out already. He wanted me to wire him money, so he could buy more of that shit. He was talking ten million miles a minute, saying he had nothing to eat, that he was starving, that he would have to sell his ass on the street if I didn't wire him anything.

No. No. No, I'll be fine. It's just…what I wanted to do was to drive down there and pick up my boy. My only son. This is my son, I kept thinking. Part of me, rotting down in that cesspool.

I told him no. I wasn't going to help him. If he wanted to come home, I would pick him up, you know? But otherwise, forget it. I wasn't going to contribute one rotten cent to his habit.

Then it was two years. We had no idea if he was dead or alive, if he was maimed or battered in some heroin hut somewhere, a needle in his ankle vein.

He was in New Mexico. He was living in the mountains, on a ranch. Homesick as hell, he wanted to come home. My son cried. He told me he loved me. Of course he was. Of course he did.

Then he gave us a bank account. He said if we wired him money, he would come back. He would.

"It's too far," he kept saying. "You can't drive out this far. I'm so sorry." I could tell he was filled with shame. This time he sounded contrite. Yeah, he actually did.

"Listen, you are my son," I told him. "That's all there is to it. Whatever you need."

Yes. We sent him the money. What else could we *do*? We *had* to send it to him.

That was the last time I heard from him. Yes, we tried that. Yes, we tried that too. We think he moved on, hitchhiked north to Alaska, down to Mexico. Wherever. Somewhere wild, out of the loop. He could be anywhere really.

I don't care about the money. I can take the time. A CFO should have some privileges, right? If you speak to him, tell him, will you? Will you tell him? How we feel. That we want him back in our life. Yes. Ask around. Please.

Yes. We'd like to wipe the slate clean. Start all over. If only I could.

III.

FLIGHTS

of FANCY

Wurlitzing

Ugly Can Be Beautiful

Harry was an ugly child. Born with a malformed right foot, Harry would shamble around the house, bracing himself against the walls for support. His mother swatted him, told him to keep his unctuous hands from smudging the walls. Each week she'd make him wipe the walls down with a faded orange sponge and bucket. Harry was also afflicted with an unfortunate face—protruding brow, eyes that seemed perpetually crossed, blotchy skin, and a thick chin. At age three his mother couldn't take it any more. "I can't even look at you," she said. "How am I expected to be your *mother*, of all things?" She gave Harry up for adoption, kissing his Neanderthal head and swiftly walking away. Harry leaned against the wall of the adoption agency for support.

A year later Mrs. Guthrie took Harry in as a foster child. Harry was gawky, but he was also smart. Though Mrs. Guthrie had two other foster children—Brianne and Nancy—he read faster, achieved better grades in school, was more able around the house. Mrs. Guthrie noticed that Harry was especially good with his hands. When her alarm clock broke Harry fixed it. When her lawnmower sputtered to a halt, Harry rewired the engine then mowed the remainder of the lawn, despite his gimpy foot. Mrs. Guthrie tried to feed Harry well, whatever dish he wanted—spaghetti and meatballs was his favorite.

Harry loved Mrs. Guthrie. Though his fuzzy memories of his biological mother often interceded, Harry needed his foster mother. She bathed him. She kneaded his swollen leg. She fended off the bullies with a baseball bat. She played the radio and sang along. Harry and Mrs. Guthrie sang together.

"You're a beautiful child," she said. "Don't let nobody tell you different."

Harry knew his foster sisters were jealous. It wasn't something Harry thought he could control. Harry wasn't fretful. He never attempted to track down his birth parents. He called Mrs. Guthrie "Mom."

9 to 5

After high school Harry found work in the local car plant working on the line. He soldered. Harry liked the sensation of being part of a team. He liked witnessing the end result—the birth of a shiny new automobile. Harry liked coming home hot and sweaty.

Mrs. Guthrie never asked Harry to move out of the house. They had conversations—Harry asked how much he would need to live on his own. Mrs. Guthrie advised him. The truth was Harry wasn't inspired to move out, even though his foster sisters already had enrolled in local colleges. He liked Mrs. Guthrie's cooking too much. Nights Harry would rest his aching left foot, soaking it in a tub of warm salt water. Mrs. Guthrie would massage it. Once, she held his mangled foot to her face, caressed it with her cheek, and kissed his toes.

"You really are a *wonderful* child," Mrs. Guthrie said.

"I'm not a child any more, Mom."

"You'll always be my child," she said.

When Harry wasn't in too much pain he would hobble down to Mrs. Guthrie's basement. Since his ninth grade shop class Harry loved metalwork. In high school Harry made picture frames, ashtrays. As an adult he worked on elaborate plant holders, desk organizers, and filing cabinets. He would give his projects away to friends. He did it for the love of the art. The sounds of Harry hammering sheet metal would make Mrs. Guthrie misty. She'd bring him peanut butter cookies and chocolate milk and watch him work under the glow of a single 75-watt bulb. Harry reminded Mrs. Guthrie of her deceased husband. Why he ever accepted the commission to that far-off war she'll never be able to reconcile.

Love Me Do

As a young man Harry was unable to approach women. Harry felt self-conscious about his backwards foot, and this halted his confidence. Mrs. Guthrie attempted to play matchmaker, but Harry was picky. He was only interested in the most beautiful women.

When Harry first saw Annabel she was working as a cashier at a clothing store in the mall, ringing up jeans and t-shirts and sweaters. The music pulsated in the store, thumping along to the beat of his heart. She was the most beautiful woman he had ever seen—doe-eyes, long and leggy, curly auburn hair thrown back over her shoulders. Her arms and hands were fine mechanisms. Harry watched her fold t-shirts on the counter, as if she were packaging a golden treasure. At the instant he saw her, Harry knew he had to speak to her, to at least try.

"You..." he said, limping to the counter. He held the edge of the counter for support. "You are..."

"I am...what?" she said. She looked away. Harry feared he had already deep-sixed his chances.

"You are...something. I'm sure of that."

Harry glanced at her nametag. "Annabel." That helped him feel more confidence. At least he knew her name.

"I am what?"

"Very pretty."

"Well, that's nice to hear," she said. "I doubt it though. What about all those supermodels and actresses?"

Harry said they were nothing compared to her, mere shadows—imitations.

"It is flattering," she said. Her face flushed and she looked at her feet. Harry could see she wore a class ring. He pegged her as nineteen.

"You're... amazing," he said.

"You are very sweet," she said.

Take a Chance with Me

Though Annabel was "dating other guys," that didn't bother Harry. Harry was ecstatic to have an opportunity to be with her, to simply look across a table and bear witness to her gorgeous face. Harry didn't feel as if he must *possess* her. Rather, he simply hoped to garner her interest enough that she might grace him with her presence again.

Harry felt silly asking this beautiful creature to accompany him to a pizza joint. Harry knew at least in theory how important first impressions can be. Tommy's pizzeria was just the natural choice. Set the bar low and who knows?

Annabel talked about her childhood, how she missed the rigors of school. She alluded to the fact that her parents never quite saw eye to eye (she blamed her mother's rigidity and primness). She told stories about pool hopping and sabotaging homecoming, even though she was the queen.

"It is a pain sometimes... to be pretty," she said, picking a mushroom off a slice of pizza.

"Too much pressure?"

"No, not that. It's too much *responsibility* really. I have to stay true to who I am?"

Harry didn't think of Annabel as self-absorbed or egotistic. She was just being factual, honest. He found her to be sweet and innocent, a woman in search of a man who understands her, who can tap into her needs.

"I want to take care of you," Harry said. "I want to take on your problems as mine. I can be very helpful."

Annabel lowered her eyes, folded her hands, and bent over her soda. Harry watched the birch beer rise through the white straw to her lips, and then suddenly descend.

"You are awfully sweet," she said.

Tupelo Honey

When they made love for the first time, Harry wept. He told Annabel that he "adored" her. In his mind he substituted "adored" for "loved." He told himself to wait to utter that word. Annabel's arms rested straight by her side, and her feet pointed at a ninety-degree angle, straight toward the ceiling. Harry flipped on a bedside fan and felt the breeze oscillate. It is good to be alive, he thought. From now on I will recognize that.

"You're not bothered by my limp?" Harry asked.

"No," Annabel said. "Your feet aren't important to me."

If Harry was one to argue he would argue this point. He

knew it wasn't worth it.

"You're not bothered by my job?"

Annabel had to ask what it is he did again.

"You think I'm beautiful," she said. "And you treat me well. That's plenty."

"Good," Harry said, breathing deeply. "Good."

Too Much of Nothing

Harry and Annabel got married after a year and they bought a small split-level in the suburbs. Annabel quit her job as a cashier and took a waitressing job instead. This gave her time during the day to make a go of her modeling career.

"You *will* make it," Harry said. He limped to her, clasped her hands and kissed them.

Harry was content. He knew how fortunate he was—so many of his friends were unmarried, searching, becoming increasingly desperate and forlorn. Harry was married to a gorgeous woman. He felt as if she was a reward for his suffering.

Annabel didn't have luck with the modeling work. She went to auditions but inevitably she was told she seemed too "stiff," or "cold," or "detached." Though they told her she was stunning, she just wasn't "open" enough.

This was difficult to swallow. Annabel was used to getting what she wanted, and she wanted to douse the world with her beauty. Annabel didn't see what the problem was: snap the camera, throw the photos out for all to see. Let the people be the judge. Who needs gatekeepers? Annabel sunk into despair.

Annabel drank.

Annabel threw vases against the wall.

Annabel called Harry a "lunk," "pathetic," "Quasimodo," and

worse. He was no longer "sweet." Harry gave her the benefit of the doubt. He knew she spoke in frustration. If anything he blamed himself. He told Annabel he would help her.

"I don't need *your* kind of assistance," she said. "Who is going to believe *you* know what is beautiful?"

Harry found solace in the basement. At all hours he could be found clanking away on his metalwork. He began to make metal representations of Annabel. He would limp up to bed, sometimes at two or three in the morning. He would curl his body into Annabel's. Annabel would turn hers away.

War Pigs

Harry usually listened to music as he worked in the basement. It helped him relax. It made him think of Mrs. Guthrie. As he worked sometimes he would smoke a cigar, drink a beer.

One night Harry had to go to a retirement party held at Trawler's, a local seafood restaurant. Expecting gifts and a speech and perhaps a band a dancing, he told Annabel he wouldn't be home until eleven. Instead, Harry felt queasy after eating his fried oyster special, and Harry apologized to Frank, his long-time colleague, and Harry drove home. When he pulled up to their house, however, Harry knew something was wrong. A large white Dodge pickup was in his driveway behind Annabel's car. The house was dark. Harry parked and opened the door.

From the landing Harry heard the sounds of feet. He heard the thumping and then saw a man in a white uniform brush through the dark kitchen out the back door. Harry knew Annabel was probably never faithful to him. Even during their engagement and early marriage he'd answer phone calls, which often ended in a click. Too many.

Still, Harry didn't get married to have his life disrupted. That was where Harry drew the line: at chaos.

Standing on the landing Harry told himself that if Annabel stepped out of the bedroom and apologized and eased his heart, he would forgive her and move on. If she didn't, Harry would take matters into his own hands. Harry gave her five minutes. He stood there looking at his watch timing her. He was sure Annabel knew he was there waiting on her. Still, she didn't move.

When five minutes were up, Harry walked out the door. He pulled his Taurus into the driveway, the spot previously occupied by the white pickup. He slept there in the car, listening to the radio softy playing. Annabel always had a thing for men in uniform.

Smoke on the Water

When Mrs. Guthrie received word from Harry, she unearthed her flashlight. Like a policeman she carried it both as a source of light and protection. She began stalking Harry's house. Whenever he wasn't around, Mrs. Guthrie was there, waiting. She looked forward to the confrontation with the man in uniform.

For weeks nothing happened. Harry sank back into his daily routine. A muted silence engulfed his home. Though they ate dinner together, their thoughts were far apart. They avoided looking at each other, and Annabel cleaned up in silence.

When Harry decided to attend a local rock concert at Red's Pub, he didn't ask Annabel. He knew she wouldn't be interested. Mrs. Guthrie was waiting, however, flashlight in hand. On patrol.

The white pickup pulled into the driveway at dusk, at the time when Harry would normally return from work. A man stepped from the truck—jeans, red T-shirt, crew cut, muscular. Mrs. Guthrie beamed her flashlight at his head. He halted, turned toward her.

"You have a problem, lady?"

Mrs. Guthrie held her flashlight in front of her. She wasn't nervous. She wasn't afraid.

"What's your name?"

"I'm not telling you my name."

"Why are you here? Who *are* you?"

"I'm not telling you that either."

"Yes, you are. Yes, you are," Mrs. Guthrie said.

She proceeded to detail the emotional wreckage he had brought about on Harry's household, how he has no right to sabotage a perfectly happy marriage, how his code of honor must be limited to his uniform (Air Force, he tells her), how his actions were illegal, punishable by law.

"A settlement is needed," she said. "Be a man."

The man narrowed his eyes at her. He didn't deny the validity of her statements. He simply shook his head in shame.

"How much then?"

"And you can't see her anymore."

He looked up at Harry's house, at the bedroom window. He nodded.

Love Child

Harry had never seen ten grand in cash in one place, but there it was rubber banded in a manila envelope. When Mrs. Guthrie handed this to him he didn't know what to say. Didn't know what to do.

So he built himself a wheelchair in the basement. Harry didn't know if it was the stress from an unfaithful wife or simply the degenerative effects of time, but his foot throbbed. With a ten thousand dollar windfall he could afford the materials for a chair.

Why not?

With the military moment of the picture, Harry felt a wave of calm overwhelm him. Even his relationship with Annabel improved. Silences were fewer. He began to see her as beautiful again, internally.

It was a Saturday afternoon. Harry had just finished mowing the lawn. For him this was an all-day project. It was especially difficult to push the mower up and down the incline. His leg didn't usually cooperate.

"I'm knocked up," Annabel said. She shook the ice in her tumbler. She didn't say much more than that.

"How far along?"

"Two months."

Harry was delighted. He wanted to be a father, wanted to raise a child with his wife. The fact that they hadn't made love since the early spring bothered Harry at first. He knew the mathematics. But the disquiet diminished. He would do unto others as they had done unto him.

"We need a celebration," Mrs. Guthrie said.

That summer they played old music on the radio, and sang along. When he closed his eyes he imagined a jukebox, churning neon. They danced some, also. It was something to behold.

Laser Eye

When Melanie told Jay she wanted to get laser eye surgery, he threw a fit. Then he chucked an open can of tomatoes across the kitchen. Melanie ducked and the can splatted against the wall behind her. Tomato juice everywhere. On the floor. On the ceiling. On the walls. On the curtains. Tomato seeds on the refrigerator. Slashed blobs of tomatoes sliding down the walls onto the floor.

"Wow, you are an asshole," Melanie yelled.

Jay said that kind of surgery was for vanity, and that they couldn't afford it. He said the whole idea creeped him out. He said he would never allow anyone to get all *Clockwork Orange* on his face. Jay stomped outside, slunk down to the dock. Melanie and Jay were staying with Melanie's mother. They couldn't afford their own apartment.

It took Melanie half an hour to clean up the mess. She knew Jay. He is just *passionate*, she thought. He is just intense. At least he isn't a slime ball cheater like the others. He can be sensitive. This is why he reacts so strongly to disappointment. A real perfectionist.

Jay was bailing out the canoe with an old Big Gulp cup. Jay didn't look up when Melanie slipped on the mossy step. He didn't turn when she shuffled to him. She patted his head and said it would be okay. She said they would work this out.

"Mom is paying for it anyway," she said. The mosquitoes hummed around them, and they slapped their legs. That summer it rained every day.

"It's nothing but a scam," he said. "They take thousands of your hard earned cash, slice your eyes up, and what are you left with? Uncertainty. How do you know it's even going to work in the first place? In the long run, I mean. How do you know it's going to last?"

"It's going to work," Melanie said. "I'm not worried about that. It will."

"So it's *faith* now?"

"No," Melanie said. "It's not faith."

"Then what is it?"

"Trust," she said. Trust, Jay thought. Instead of trusting me, she trusts the laser eye doctors. Who next? The butcher? The baker? The ice cream maker? Jay knew he always gave his all to Melanie. One hundred percent. One hundred and thirty percent. Jay wondered: what percent of herself does she give me? Sixty or seventy tops. And I'm a very successful paralegal. I could do much better if I wanted. *Much* much better. Then again… a bird in hand.

Melanie bent down next to Jay and submerged her hands in the canoe water. She cupped her hands and splashed the water into the lake, helping him bail. Jay slapped a mosquito on his right thigh. Melanie slapped her neck. Melanie hated letting him down. She knew she wasn't vain, but Jay was making her feel that way. She hated these guilt trips.

"Are you really going to take this thing out there now? It's so buggy."

"I don't have a problem with a few bugs. That's reality. Reality is bugs. Reality is glasses, not some futuristic *Blade Runner* laser eye bullshit. I can adjust," he said.

As Melanie splashed the water out of the canoe with her hands, she watched Jay fill the cup and dump fountain after murky fountain of water into the lake. Melanie wondered: what will my life be like when I'm thirty? Where will I be living? What will I be doing? Hopefully not still working at CPI Industries processing data. This is why I went to college? All those history and anthropology and philosophy classes for this? I would be less bored staring at a brick wall for eight hours.

Jay watched the water stream from the red cup to the lake itself. Why does she bother? If she really wanted to help she would go back up there and get a bucket, he thought. What's the point of this stupid doggy paddle bullshit splashing? She's just trying to make *herself* feel better. It's just like the laser eye thing: she doesn't know the way the world works. She's just following a line that some "friend" handed her. I know her, Jay thought. She'll regret it later. Jay imagines queues of laser eye surgery victims waiting surgeons to give them their "real" eyes back.

When the canoe was dry they looked up at each other. Melanie knew that if she didn't get in the boat with him that would be it. If he didn't invite her into the canoe, she would leave him. If he didn't invite her, he was more interested in his pride, more interested in his stubborn self-exploration than the compromise it took to maintain a relationship. This was a simple litmus test. Cut and dry.

Jay lifted the front end of the canoe and turned his head vaguely towards Melanie. If she goes ahead with the surgery, Jay thought, she isn't the woman I want to be with anyway. What's next? A boob job? Liposuction? And if she doesn't get in the canoe with me, Jay thought, forget it.

"Can you help me get this down?"

Melanie nodded and grabbed the other end. It wasn't a heavy canoe, and the water level was high. They dropped the boat directly into the water. Jay tossed one oar into the boat and slipped into the hull.

"So you're going alone then?"

Jay nodded. Melanie slapped her neck. Jay slapped his arm. Melanie nodded. Jay nodded.

"Got to face down these mosquitoes someday," he said. "Right?"

"Whatever you say," Melanie said, snorting. "Good luck with that."

Jay pushed off with his oar, and Melanie sat on the edge of the dock, watching his wake shimmy left to right. Melanie watched the cloud of mosquitoes that followed him over the water. Jay slapped at his neck and head and the canoe shimmied. Melanie watched the wake ripple and lap against the rocks and roots and decomposing leaves and mud. The shore absorbed the ripples and the water calmed.

On the Coast

I'm on the edge of the berm, learning slack key guitar from my ex-wife. After three years she's back from Hawaii. Her eyes are webbed. Gina wears stilettos these days, but we're still close. We could never work it out in the right way. I blame myself. I haven't been employed in a year. Not since the dredging job. Ever since we split, I can't seem to get motivated. I think of it as midlife temporary retirement. More useful than waiting for the onset of Alzheimer's.

"Slick Willy," she says, showing me where to place my fingers on the struts. I nod. "It's the name of a song," she says. She has the voice of a radio personality, without a trace of grating salsyness. She's not a glad-hander. Her voice reminds me of nectarines.

"I view my life as an eddy," I say. "Not a lake."

"Not a lake," she replies, and holds my hand to the frets. I love the way she repeats my words. Gina's got my goat, or is it "goad"? She has a bag of pears propped between her feet. I can smell her dandelion perfume. I'm thinking of words. Esplanade. Coquina. Epoxy. I'd like to quote Pascal and E.M. Cioran, but that would be pretentious. God forbid pretensions.

My fingers are making music, but she's guiding me. Her new husband is asleep inside on the hammock, a sitcom on a low hum. We all get along to the best of our ability. The child we share—our child—splashes in the misty water below. The waves lap flaccidly against the rocks. Gulls guffaw unseen above. Welcome to my coastline, I think. I lean back into Gina, feel her hair against the back of my neck. Welcome to this, I think, back to the remainder of it.

Homing

"Lets gv a little sht-out for Js. Whoo whoo." I click enter, post. It's up. I don't really believe sixty, seventy percent of what I write up there. I do it. Save face. Buggers.

Ninety second later Elmer posts, "I cn fl the luv, boooooy. Prs t lrd. Whut, whut." He's a yes man. Emily chimes in, per usual.

I watch, learn. My parents are always out there. They don't have a gauge (the blog doesn't help). If only I had a sister or brother. Not so lucky in that department. In the living-in-a-nine-bedroom-McMansion-department I'm doing just fine. Meadow Haven Way.

My goal: getting out of Dodge altogether—Dodge being my own personal five hundred square feet trap.

For once I'd like to have a conversation with someone I can trust, someone who isn't *selling* me something. Actually, if I could garner this I'd forget the rest. When I went to Rockpark Elementary, I did. That was for one year, first grade—before my parents decided to pull out, go the homeschool route. Lucky, lucky me.

I can only stand the blog for ten minutes at a time. Moronic. Some of these homers are on constantly (nothing else better to do). I watch them at our weekly "assessment session" down at the Y. They have their Bluetooth earpieces, their Smartphones or Crackberries, their Holy Bible in protective gear. Me—I usually need a ride to and fro.

Last meeting I knitted. I got some oddball looks, but as I told them, "There's nothing faggy about knitting booties." It's my niece after all. They clutch and type faster. Jesus' cyborgs.

I change into my God Bless America t-shirt, hide my knitting cubby, open the door for my mother. It's eight thirty-seven. Father will come home after ten—zoning meeting. My parents are busy constructing Loudoun County. They don't mind one bit of controversy. Sometimes I think they search it out.

"Hey there, kitten," she says. She scruffs my hair, hands me a six inch sub from Jerry's.

"Hey, Mom," I say.

"Tzunkudo already made me a French omelet and spring potatoes." Tru.

"Just in case you get puckish," she says. Mom is wearing a mint green power suit. She looks like she belongs on an ice cream cone.

She pats my head again, says she's going to change into something comfortable. This is code language for "I'm going to plant myself in front of the Internet." I don't see her again that night.

On CL I post a plea for a "friend" who can't "indulge in conversation." Someone to talk to, pls. I cross my fingers for a non-sexual response. I even knock twice on the HB.

The concept behind homing is 365 school. Integrating my life with my learning. The cyborgs would say non-homers wouldn't get it, I suppose. They could: it's just different. I put in two, maybe three hours of work per day—but it's project-based.

I harvest ideas. Winter to spring to summer to fall.

I write a lot in my head.

I am an observer of transience.

For instance, Tzunkudo. Mother calls him our "servant," but I wonder. Sethy thinks he's working for free under obligation. "You're a slave owner," he says. "Free the Israelites." Sethy only e-mails when he's not helping his parents muck stalls. Thoroughbreds take upkeep, he says. What doesn't?

I try to converse with Tzunkudo, but his vocabulary is somewhere in the range of one hundred words. He's probably a genius though: all I have to do is point to a picture of a dish and he creates it.

We played checkers once. I taught him the game with no verbal instruction—just pointing and examples. He won by a far margin.

One day he will decide he doesn't like sleeping in our old Y2K shelter, high-tail it for the foothills. I won't say a thing.

I receive seventeen replies to my desperate CL plea, all of them old pervos with photographic accompaniment.

The one human response reads as follows: "Hiya, kiddo. Sure, let's chat. Starbucks? What's your favorite position?"

That's it. I realize this response isn't exactly the Algonquin Roundtable. Still, it's something to hang my hat on for a day.

The next morning I respond: "Dear Hiya kiddo person: yes, Starbucks. 7:30 tm?"

Yes, smiley face response in two minutes tops. I like an opportunity.

In the meantime I study rooms of the famous on the Internet. And I knit.

Marci posts on the blog: "Certain some1 needs 2 rmbr wr all in ths tgthr." I know she means me. Marci psychologically bats her eyelashes at me upon each visit. I try to tell her I'm not depressed, that I'm not a snob, that meeting every day is not my idear of phun, much less Homing. What's the point?

I try to relate this to Tzunkudo. He stares and me as he whips cream to top off the freshly baked apricot pie. I do the checker piece sign in the air. He holds up a singular finger. We have communicated.

Once I tried to ask him where he's from. That was a waste of time. Mother says Djibouti, but Father says Ivory Coast. But who really knows?

I hail a taxi with twenty-dollars of my $1250 monthly allowance. The driver is Serbian and wants to talk soccer.

"Bleck," I say. "Sports."

"You no like sports? What wrong with you?"

I begin knitting. His face is as pursed as a raisin. He wants nothing to do with me except my twenty dollars. I watch faces so I know.

"Kiddo?" I scan the room. It's the chubby woman in the lime green track suit. Orange stripes up her thighs.

"Star," she says. She's sitting in a brown Starbucks armchair, wrists dangling off each arm.

"Nice to meet you," I say.

"Ditto," she says.

She sips her coffee and I sit in front of her. I feel as if I'm in a job interview. She watches the bridge of my nose. I can feel her eyes hover above mine.

I like studying faces—a lost art. Hers is pineapple shaped with reddish freckles. Her eyes are green, but I'd bet they're tinted contact lenses. Her hair is frizzy, pulled back with a scrunchie thing. She wears an olive skirt, black boots, wine-colored long sleeve shirt. She's impassive. I'd guess she's thirty. I'm not good with ages though; I'm too young.

"Star, huh?" I'm trying to fathom what she's after.

"Nickname," she says. "You know how it is—just latched onto it. Or *it* latched onto me."

"Yeah," I say. Kitten, for starters.

Star offers to buy me a coffee, and she does, and I drink it. I expect her to be a foot fetishist, or worse…much.

The coffee is burnt, as usual, with an ammonia smell. It tastes like cat pee smells.

Turns out she's not a foot fetishist.

I tell her about homing, knitting, rooms of the famous. She tells me about climbing trees, coloring, word searches. She's into "reclaiming her childhood." She doesn't believe in "infantalization," just allowing herself "liberty." "Free as the birds, free," she says.

Since she's interested I tell her about the time my mother drove me into the mountains. I'm still not one hundred percent sure why, but I was small and slept in the back of the mini-van. When I woke up, we drove through foothills. I asked her where we were, and she just smiled. She drove for a long time, and then my mother came to a cabin, told me to stay in the car. I did as she told me to. "I couldn't help kicking the seat after fifteen minutes though. She was inside with someone. I couldn't see through the curtains. I just had to wait. When she came back to the car my mother said we are lost. She didn't know where we were. I watched a triangular gap in the curtains open as she talked. Her forehead was sweaty.

Star barely blinks as I recount this memory. I tell Star I'm not sure what it means, if anything. I tell her maybe I'm misremembering what really happened.

"I doubt it," Star says.

I don't want to leave the coffee shop. Star left. The dwellers left. The baristas cleaned up. I sit there in the chair where Star sat listening. Lucky me.

We promised to IM. I told her I'd give her access to the kid perspective. Funny since I don't know if I have one.

The taxi picks me up within five minutes and I am home before my parents. On the cab ride back I think of all the things I can do to make a change—run off to the hinterlands, send Tzunkudo on his way, elope with Star.

Instead, I sit on my bed and knit. I'm not thinking of Underground Railroad quilt cryptograms exactly, but I do want to make a statement. A great black plus sign on a field of white. Plus, not cross.

The Make Out Club

The Make Out Club meets every Wednesday night at nine. When we meet in Johnny's basement, the lava lamps are already fizzing and churning at full bubble. We make our own in Priscilla's garage. Red, blue, green, orange, yellow. We are all untarnished.

Johnny says the best way to gain control of your life is to put your tongue down someone else's throat. Luke says the phrase "tonsil-hockey" is so 20th Century. He likes the phrase "snakes in a cave." We switch off frequently. Two or three minutes, then dosy-do. We play emo not screamo, drink birch beer instead of real beer.

"I.M. me tonight," I say.

"You I.M. me," Hillary jeers. I can feel her pessimism radiate. She's a real vortex. We make out for two, but her tongue flaps around like a dying perch. It doesn't do what a tongue should do. My tits are bigger than hers, so she thinks she has a right to more than her share. The boys like her better, even though she's only twelve. I suspect she has broken the pledge. But when ice coats the trees, outside isn't a possibility. Even in cars, it's difficult unless you keep the engine running. But none of us are old enough for that.

The power has gone out three times in the last week. This doesn't hurt our chances. We've discussed the possibility of meeting more frequently. We need one more "aye" to make a majority of eleven.

We have to finish by a quarter of ten and hit the roads. That's when Johnny's father comes home from the hospital. We carpool. Our parents come. They think we have a math club in the works.

Tim's got his hand down my pants, and I can see him stiffen. Tim's the favorite one. Even Seth and Otto keep their fingers crossed for two minutes with him. In the orange glow near the bean bag Hillary is on top of Ed. She's acting like he's a prize, like I should be jealous. I can see her eyes on Tim though. She's biding her time. When the egg timer goes off, we put our numbers back in the bag and draw. I'm hoping for Tim again, or maybe Nick. I get eight. Tiffany. Hillary yelps. She has Tim now. Tim rolls his eyes, and I feel a surge of vindication. Johnny resets the timer. I can feel the bass throb in my stomach.

Nobody knows why they targeted Lakeland Middle that day. They just did. It's just a fact that sits there, like a boulder in a field. I don't remember the shots or the seared smell. I don't remember the police. The screams. The sirens. Blood. I swear I don't remember a thing.

Tiffany holds my face in her hands, presses herself to me. She's flat, but I don't mind. Her tongue dances in my mouth, bobbing like an elegant fish. For two minutes she's all I ever hoped for. Then it's over.

The Pastry Chef

So, my stepsister Alice. She divorces her husband of ten years. Bart. High school sweethearts. Sad, sad, sad. Claims he beat her. Wins 75% in court. Unheard of, her lawyer says. But abuse factored in. So she said. I don't know what to believe, but I don't believe her. Bart was a good guy. He moves out to Lexington, Kentucky to start all over. Wants to live out in the hills, somewhere he can find himself again. Don't blame him one bit. Would do the same if I was him. I still call him. Don't ask him about the beatings, but if I did I would trust his answer.

Alice says she wants to meet a sensitive man. An artist. A teacher. A dancer. An editor. A musician. Something of this ilk. I try to tell her that a job doesn't make a man sensitive. Won't make him better than Bart. I tell her she's restless. She tells me where to go. She wants to wear the pants. Big time. Funny thing is she's 5'1 and one hundred pounds, little candy corn teeth. But she's got lip. She's got sass. And a temper. She always had that.

Five weeks after the divorce, Alice meets this pastry chef, Seth. She's in her stilettos on some fashionable street when this Seth makes a sophisticated pass at her. He's tall, strapping, charming. She calls me up to tell me. Makes him sound like God's gift to women. Tells me on their first date the guy sat her down with a glass of

Glenturret, played Lester Young on the stereo, made her goat cheese popovers, marmalade croissants and bannocks. Said she just about came right there at his breakfast bar. Next time they are into each other hot and heavy.

"He's a pastry chef," Alice says. "What more could I ask for? He works at one of the fanciest restaurants in town. I'm talking five star. I mean, there are only two five star restaurants in the entire state, and he's the pastry chef at one of them. It's like dating a professional athlete, you know. He's the cream of the crop. I'm like his groupie, and I don't even mind. And he is *such* a sweetheart."

I told her this is all well and good, but what is he like? Does Seth seem like a good person? Does he seem like the kind of guy she wants to settle down with? Does he seem like someone she can trust? If he has one groupie, who's to say he doesn't have more?

"Jesus, Meredith," she says. "You're not listening. He's making me chocolate éclairs next week. I love watching him finger the dough."

So Alice dresses up in all black. Heals. Pearls. The works. Takes her to the finest Turkish restaurant in town, then back to his place for éclairs and more. They make passionate love. He tells her he loves her, that he wants to father her children. She's swept away. It's the greatest night of her life. Fine.

Six months later she's getting hitched to Seth. Alice moves into Seth's 5,000 square feet spread. My husband Gary and I go to the wedding, but we don't have to agree with the course of events. With the violent pace. I shake Seth's hand. He winks at me. Reminds me of one of those dolls. His eyes look like they are made of glass. Who does this guy think he is? My husband winces.

He doesn't want kids, and Alice is fine with this, since she's thirty four already. Doesn't want to push the envelope. It's enough to have Kenny from her ex, she says. I wonder if she has sour grapes. Everybody knows second marriages need that glue. Custody isn't enough. What does Seth care about that?

Two months after the wedding Alice sends me an invite to come over for tea with her and Seth. Says "P.S.—The Pastry Chef will, of course, give us something to munch upon. Apricot scones, if we're lucky!" I go, sans Gary. Most guys couldn't give a shit about tea. Especially second rate accountants. And when we were married I thought accountants were first cousins to lawyers. Gary would rather scratch his jock strap, watch golf. Or play golf. This is his life. Our marriage is about a dimpled white ball. "Life is a game," he once said. Considers that depth. Some motto. I'm just an accompaniment.

Alice lets me in. Figured I should bring something light, so I brought a can of Del Monte pineapple. Alice thanked me, immediately slipped it into the pantry nook. Didn't appreciate this one bit. Gary doesn't make that much money after all. *He's* not a pastry chef. Can't even reheat Kraft mac and cheese to save his life.

So I'm over there at Alice's 5,000 square footage, in the sun room drinking chamomile and gnawing on an admittedly delicious scone—black currant (though Seth has a spread of five choices). Seth holds Alice's face in his hands. Kisses the tip of her nose. She beams. They show me pictures from their three-week honeymoon in New Zealand. Nauseating.

When Alice is in the can Seth winks at me again. Want to ask him about that, but don't. Want to scratch the surface of this guy, but find a way to hold back. This is about being an adult, sharing my happiness for their union.

"I'm very happy for both of you," I say. I pinch the corners of my mouth, like they taught me to do during school pictures.

"Are you?" Seth says. He sips his tea. I clap my mouth. I'm

not saying another word. I let the silence seep in. "I'm glad to hear that," he says, and half-winks to end the exchange. He asks me if I want another scone. That's a dig. I look at the tray of perfection. Listen to Alice clink in the kitchen. Think about knocking it onto the floor, watch the pastry chef on all fours, dusting off his creations. Then I realize they probably have a maid on call.

Alice stands at the doorway with a glass of seltzer. Organic lemon wedge floating in the clinking glass. The sun emerges from behind a cloud, unleashing light upon us. The angle is revealing. In the sun I can see blemishes on Alice's nose, on Seth's forehead. A pimple. A small ugly white scar. This is enough for now, I think. I drain the dregs of my cup of tea. Stand into the light, and walk inside to blast the water, sit on the closed toilet. Hold my head in my hands and flush. Let the sounds of the water clean me out. Something has to.

Indigo

The man in the Havelock fidgets with his crochet project. He's making a blanket for his niece, but it isn't coming out right. He stares at the Brooks' mansard roof, sings along to The Isley Brothers. That falsetto. His phone brays off and on, but he doesn't answer—he's screening his calls.

His name is Edward, but he goes by "Indigo." As a young man he felt a nickname would help. Aura. Indigo never married. He was always shy. The men at the office think he's a twit. Indigo doesn't care. His job is just a job. It's only Windsor chairs. Indigo finds fulfillment elsewhere. Keep it simple he tells himself. Simple.

When he closes his eyes Indigo imagines grottoes, cuttlefish gliding through brackish water, casabas on marble, vibraphones in the sleet, buxom scullery maids dancing in the blue light. He opens his eyes. Back to his crochet.

The fact that he sits in a football stadium filled with fans is just a coincidence. For Indigo, where he places his rump is insignificant. Men and women cheer. The loudspeakers blare. Men in blue chase men in orange and then vice versa. I will not be nullified, Indigo thinks. I will not be made obsolete. He finishes the blanket. He will send it off tomorrow. You're only alone if you believe you are.

At night he writes letters by hand, licks stamps, seals envelopes. The missives go to distant cousins and pen pals and long lost friends. Indigo believes in these quiet human exchanges. He learns things this way: his fourth cousin Kim is a professor of oology; his friend Nelson was convicted of racketeering; his great-aunt, Melba, had a tiff with his grandmother. For dinner Indigo parboils potatoes and cabbage. That's it.

Indigo wears chamois to bed. His lucky, crooked linstock rests above his bed on two parallel nails. The photo of his great-great grandfather's hansom carriage hangs on the wall opposite. Propped against the far corner is his miniature alpenhorn. On his bed stand: a green pocket-sized bible, reading glasses, a mug of water. Lights off, fan on; Indigo smells the musty room. He cocoons himself in blankets. It isn't difficult, Indigo thinks. Don't overthink.

Leisure

The ache in his tooth aches like no other ache he has ever felt, and in fact, the ache isn't even an ache, more like a tug, a pull boat or trawler that trolls inside his gums and jaw for pain, a pain that comes in bursts, in Alexander Calder vividness, in crimson spurts that ache or tug.

He always thought history advanced in a straight line, perhaps meandering, wavering, halting, pausing, but always more or less straight in a crooked manner, nevertheless advancing to the beat of a timpani, with rotating rounds of piccolo and oboe in accompaniment: but recently he realized this is not so.

"Because wholeness is what man strives for, the power to achieve leisure is one of the fundamental powers of the human soul."

Today is an aviary day, one of the three days when he must attend to the egrets, and the Acadian flycatchers, the buffalohead ducks, and the dowitchers, the lazuli buntings, and the Sandhill cranes, the American bittern, and the avocets, the scaled quail, and the pine siskin.

His mother used to say if he wasn't working more than forty hours a week, he wasn't maximizing his potential, as his worth is quantifiable, as he was to be productive and reasonable, and reproductive, and rational: he wonders what she would make of him now, not that he would change regardless, or could—not that he is in any way remarkable in his own eyes—or that these thoughts stick with him like the thumping ache of his tooth.

The tooth is one of the back teeth, which he thinks is a molar (perhaps he is wrong), but he will live with the pain rather than go to the dentist, for dentists spend all day with their hands in people's mouths, and who can respect a man, or a woman, who would chose to spend all day with their hands in people's mouths?

Not that his line of work is superior (clearly it is not), and he doesn't think of it as a line really, but just something to divert him from his usual activities—plus he likes the birds and the cafeteria does occasionally grant him free hotdogs and pretzels, as many as he wants.

He must wake up since the alarm has gone off ten times, and ten times he has hit snooze, and he's supposed to be there at nine thirty and already it's eight forty five which will leave little time for a frozen bagel and/or instant coffee.

"The religious value set upon constant, systematic, efficient work in one's calling as the ready means of securing the certainty of salvation and of glorifying God became a most powerful agency in economic expansion."

History advances, if "advances" is the right word, in a figure eight, looping back to its origins and then back around to its opposite.

The birds help him realize this.

He has a feeling of fainting, though he is still lying in bed, but still the feeling continues, as if he's falling *though* the bed, into the box springs, through the box springs, under the floor, under the bedrock, into the mantle of the Earth, and melting in the flow of lava or whatever it is called when it is in the mantle of the Earth.

Then the feeling passes.

Bzzzzzzzzzzzzzzzzzzzzzzzz.

Eleven.

He thinks of the roadrunner, nothing like the Warner Brothers roadrunner, evading the cartoon coyote.

He thinks of connectivity: the soul of the alarm clock, the soul of his mother, the soul of the Ex-lax, the soul of the Jell-o, the soul of the credit card, the soul of the Dixie cups, each one with its own soul.

These are overwhelming thoughts that, at times, precede the fainting, and at other times inspire him to retreat into himself where he can connect with the souls and sift through the connectedness.

"Leisure, it must be clearly understood, is a mental and spiritual attitude—it is not simply the result of external factors, it is not the inevitable result of spare time, a holiday, a weekend or a vacation."

The roadrunner is sick with something, which he should bring to the attention of the zookeeper, but he wonders if the zookeeper will question him, as he usually does by saying: "Why didn't you bring this to my attention earlier?"

The soul of the roadrunner is unique, and independent, which he can *feel* more than see, and which feels like a cat's whiskers on the back of his thighs.

Perhaps the figure eight doesn't truly loop back around, since a gap may exist somewhere along the loop, and if this is so, how do events connect to one another or cause one another at all? You can't understand these things just by reading, he thinks.

The feeling of fainting comes to him when he is stressed, which is what he tried to explain to his mother, but she wanted him to see a doctor for this, which he couldn't do as a result of his many feelings of anxiety and remorse, though his mother wanted him to explain these matters to her, which he had a difficult time doing.

The toothache is no longer a tooth ache, but a jaw ache, a face ache, a skull ache.

Vibrations ripple through his jaw, and face, and skull as the alarm goes off again.

Bzzzzzzzzzzzzzzzzzzzzzzzz.

Twelve.

"Compared with the exclusive ideal of work as activity, leisure implies (in the first place) an attitude of non-activity, of inward calm, of silence; it means not being 'busy' but letting things happen."

He thinks of the soul of the zookeeper, the soul of his tooth, the soul of erector sets, the sun, blenders, grass.

He thinks he should now get up, for if he doesn't he might be fired, and if he's fired he will not be able to take care of the birds, and if he's not able to take care of the birds another soul will, a soul that may or not be as intimately attuned to the souls of birds as his soul.

If the figure eight doesn't loop back around and connect—which he is more and more certain it doesn't—then events are just events, and are flat and drained of meaning: and if this is so, the Ruby-crowned Kinglet is a philosopher for soaring above the conifers of Alaska.

"In his well-known study of capitalism Max Weber quotes the saying, that 'one does not work to live; one lives to work,' which nowadays no one has much difficulty in understanding: it expresses the current opinion."

Yet when he verbalizes this to his other half, she tells him his mother was right—he *is* depressed.

Yet he has never abused drugs and/or alcohol, and he has a

sunny disposition.

Can people with sunny dispositions still be depressed?

Perhaps this has something to do with his tooth.

He thinks he should now get up because it will feel nice to have warm jets of water rushing over his body.

He unplugs the alarm clock, thinks about trying a mental approach, and then he feels as if he might faint again, but it passes, though the skull ache persists like a xebec over the rough waters of the Indian Ocean.

The apartment is still warm from yesterday, and even naked he begins to sweat—another reason to initiate the jets of water.

His other half has left one wet towel on the floor, a green one, the faded green one the color of baby lettuce.

He steps into the hot jets of water and sighs.

He wonders if the shower has a soul, then he feels it; then he wonders if water has a soul or if each particle of water has its own soul, but he thinks it is just water, all water. A single soul for all water, rather than a collection of little individual soul molecules.

The roadrunner will be happy to see him, happier than the neediest lunatic child.

History is an oxymoron, he thinks, an artificial projection of meaning onto what truly is chaos.

He thinks of the soul of his other half, which he is unsure about, and the soul of the timpani and Alexander Calder, and 'God Bless America,' and 'Autumn Leaves' if songs have souls—which he thinks they do.

Perhaps the dentist isn't such a bad idea. He can always reconceptualize.

He dries off with a pink towel the color of penicillin.

"Man, then, is limited by his environment in exactly the same way as an animal, that is to say, he is limited to a selected environment assembled, as it were, by natural selection and biological necessity; he is incapable of apprehending anything and, even though searching for it, of finding anything outside his environment—like the jackdaw that cannot find a motionless grasshopper."

Or a frozen bagel, since his other half cleaned the refrigerator. Thin pickings.

But the happiness of the roadrunner isn't happiness, he knows.

His mother used to wonder if he could find contentment, but he would always tell her that contentment isn't there to find, that contentment finds us.

Instead, he eats a piece of ice chomping it into bits, letting water dribble down his jaw.

This doesn't help matters.

And if history is an oxymoron, then forget the aviary, though there are consequences that will have to be attended to.

Perhaps he'll go to the park instead, though if he goes to the park instead of the zoo perhaps he will not eat anything all day, which will not do since like the Western Grebe, we have to eat.

His mother probably thought he was an odd child.

He decides to go to work, and decides to dress, as the children may be startled to see him naked when he tends to the birds.

"Whatever the laxity of the law, the Christian is bound to consider the golden rule and the public good."

If it were only so simple, he thinks, my life would be much easier.

Yes, yes, yes, yes, yes, yes.

He opens the door, and locks it behind him, thinking of the

soul of the ice cube, and the soul of the doorknob, and his shirt, and the bird shit he will scrape, the seed he will offer, and how these things are all as interlaced as a basket—thatchery.

Perennial

He has a need to please, a real mothering instinct. No one must leave unfulfilled.

He is born each year in the last March snow, the crocuses lancing through the warming humus. He roasts spits of lamb with asparagus and baby carrots. Glasses of pinot noir clink. Heads roll and toss. Music trumpets. The moon rises and pales in the thinning mist. Guests waltz down the esplanade and blow kisses to each other in the morning dew.

The air warms with growth. Gnats circle amongst the saplings. Buds and shoots emerge. The women in his life come to. The one with raven hair calls his name in the afternoon; the shorter one crouches over him, freckled and sweet; the lanky muscular woman pins his arms to the loam. If he had the time, he would marry each one.

Oh, the scents of tomatoes and cantaloupe. Mosquitoes and beetles and moths cloud the street lamps. The water slaps against the dock in the moonlight and the women dive into the water. A tang of salt lingers on the lips. He invites them all to celebrate the heat and long nights, and they come. They drink chardonnay and ale, and laugh, and roll in the warm grass, alive and well. He feels seasoned and languorous. He watches them all and leans back, hands behind his head. The pinprick of expectancy can wait.

The crickets moan, and the frost stiffens the grass and plants. Only a few come, and they arrive late, as if they aren't sure. They eat squash and what's left of the onions and peppers. He sighs in cinnamon. Leaves hiss through the branches when they depart. His bones ache. The wind gusts: a scar of loneliness.

They don't come any more. He invites them, but it is too cold, too icy. The twinge of death hovers, in the air. He feels ancient, withering. The snow falls and layers upon itself. Heavy with ice, branches crack and fall to earth. The flowers seem distant, never to return. Holding his chest, he reclines. The blankets. Steam. His toes are icy to the touch.

When he dies they blink and nod and warm their hands by the fire. They know in a few months he will return. They know each year he blooms, a perennial lurking in the thick hump of soil.

Bendering the Spoon

When she gave birth, she didn't expect it to be a spoon. But it was a normal teaspoon. She looked at the round head and held the handle. The handle was decorated with a filigree of ivy that swooped up and down the handle. The mother ran her thumb down the ivy. The spoon was moist but silent. Perhaps it needed a drawer.

The new mother washed and rinsed her baby spoon and slipped her teaspoon into an athletic sock and transferred the other spoons to the section of the drawer that held the forks. The forks and ordinary spoons could share. It wasn't as if there was anybody else to care. Thank you very much. Single motherhood to a teaspoon would be no picnic.

When she went to bed that night she didn't hear a peep from her teaspoon. She wondered if the drawer was too confining. She wondered if she could bend the teaspoon by simply thinking about it. She didn't know if she had the mental strength.

The new teaspoon quickly became her favorite for stirring coffee, for eating yogurt, and cereal. The spoon was deeper than the other spoons, that much better for scooping vegetable soup and the like. The new mother loved her teaspoon so much she thought of buying a frame and hanging the spoon on the wall. But this would defeat the purpose of functionality.

Increasingly, when she put the teaspoon in her mouth, she noticed that the teaspoon seemed to vibrate with little humming noises. The new mother had heard of glasses of water doing this on their own, but she would never give birth to a glass of water. Not even a coffee mug really.

The next year the mother was astounded to realize she was pregnant again. She didn't know how that would happen when she was so immersed in eating with her teaspoon.

"But you are," the doctor said.

"But how?" the mother asked.

"I'm sure you're the expert on that," the doctor said.

"Very funny," the mother said.

When the doctor showed the mother the sonogram it revealed that the mother would give birth to a beautiful baby bowl. The bowl was of the soup and cereal variety, the doctor explained. Not a pasta bowl. The doctor's forehead was marked with small rivulets, like dry creek beds. The mother found him to be reasonably attractive for a genial family doctor.

"Have you often seen baby bowls?" the mother asked.

"Oh, sure. You have nothing to worry about."

"Just like the teaspoon."

"Same deal," the doctor said.

The teaspoon and bowl got along famously. The young mother began keeping the teaspoon in the bowl. The bowl didn't seem to mind. Sometimes she would place them on the windowsill, sometimes on the counter in the sun. She liked to watch the sun glint off the base of the spoon. She wondered if she could balance the spoon on the tip of her nose.

Sometimes the mother would place the spoon and the bowl in the dishwasher together. Give them a whirl. The spoon always came out shiny and buoyant. Sometimes food particles stuck to the lip of the bowl. If she didn't turn the bowl upside down it would collect water. For fun the mother liked to place the teaspoon face-to-face with another spoon. This was called playing the spoons. She had seen men do this, though usually they were dressed in dirty overalls. She didn't own overalls and she was terrible at keeping a beat.

When the teaspoon sat in the bowl, the mother knew they would all have a good day. The spoon and bowl never cried or carried on when they were together, and the mother didn't have to marry. The spoon and bowl never cried or carried on anyway, but the mother knew that any day now the teaspoon would hit its terrible twos. She wasn't sure, developmentally speaking, what that meant. The mother wanted to be prepared for anything: bending, tarnishing, dripping.

From the library the mother took out copies of books on how to care for silverware. She couldn't find a thing on bowls, but the mother assumed the bowl would fall in line. The mother bought silverware polish and used her best rag to make her teaspoon squeaky clean. Afterward, she would treat them both with a heaping bowl of chicken noodle soup—their favorite.

When the woman discovered she was pregnant again, she returned to the doctor's office. The rivulet-lined face stared at her once again. This time, she didn't see a trace of a smile.

"You are going to be the proud mother of a cute baby fork."

"A fork? But what about the tines?"

"The tines might cause some complications," the doctor said. "Of course, it all depends on the delivery."

"Right."

"You want the handle to emerge first, obviously. Not the first."

"Obviously."

The woman was so disturbed by her new baby, she became easily distracted. The mother began to dream of cutlery, of tableware. She dreamt of a melting spoon next to a melting clock in the desert. She didn't know why this was happening to her of all people: she always preferred finger food.

It was bound to happen. One day after eating a bowl of oatmeal, the mother dropped the spoon and bowl. The spoon bounced from the floor, sending a glob of oatmeal splattering against the counter. The bowl didn't have it so lucky. The bowl cracked in half. The oatmeal seeped down onto the kitchen floor in between the cracks.

The mother lifted the spoon and the cracked bowl. The spoon she washed off and stuck in the dishwasher. The mother wasn't so sure what to do with the bowl. She doubted if the emergency room would even consider a broken bowl an emergency. She decided to do her own triage. She washed out the wound, and then attempted to use to glue the bowl back together. A crusty tube of Superglue was all she had on hand. This would have to do. The mother could hear the spoon vibrating mournfully in the dishwasher. Poor little tyke. The mother tried bending the spoon. Then she tried Bendering the spoon. This went nowhere.

The mother pressed the two halves of the bowl together for what must have been half an hour, but after all her efforts the bowl would not stick. The glue was too weak. The mother was confronted with her new reality: the teaspoon would have to be her sole consolation.

When she called the funeral home to inquire about a service for her broken bowl, the man said he would be happy to assist her in the preparations in any way. Two days later the mother stood over the coffin of the young bowl and watched the man shovel dirt onto the lid. The young mother held flowers in one hand and her spoon in the other. She could feel the tiny fork tines poking her.

The mother's consolation was that she gave birth to a bouncing baby fork. The fork and spoon got along very well, though at times she had to separate them on opposite sides of the plate. The young mother could only hope for a knife next. That way she would have the beginnings of a whole table setting. That would be something.

The Walker

Lyn was a walker. She liked walking.

When she was a child she never took the bus. She always walked.

After college she found a job in the city. She walked everywhere. When she took vacations she would hike up mountains, walk ancient cities.

She would usually walk alone. Lyn attributed her loneliness to walking. Men would hoot and whistle at her: "Get in the car, baby! Nice ass! Whoo—shake it!"

Lyn wasn't interested in the role of passenger. Lynn enjoyed being alone with her thoughts, walking with them, carrying them around with her.

When Lyn dreamed, the landscape slowly scrolled by at three miles an hour.

Lyn loved to work out her dialing problems while she walked. Lyn loved the feel of the ground moving beneath her. When she was walking Lyn felt connected.

Lyn's parents died of old age three months a part. When she quit her job in the city, Lyn decided she needed a vacation. A long vacation with lots of walking, time for reflecting. She was forty-two. She had plenty of time.

When Lyn heard that one could walk from New York to Texas by following the power lines, she thought this sounded worthwhile.

So she did it. She sublet her apartment. She stopped her mail. Dumped her mediocre boyfriend. The relationship wasn't going anywhere anyway. She knew they were stuck in the rigidity of their middle-aged personalities. Lyn knew she wasn't good at handling human ambiguity. She didn't feel like working at something indistinct and intangible. Walking was the opposite: it was grounded.

Lyn packed her backpack, her tent, her clothes, food. She set out for Texas, following the power lines. It was difficult to get lost this way, Lyn thought. It was easy to slip into automatic pilot. It was almost as if the power lines did the walking for her, as if they were a train track.

In the back of her mind Lyn worried about the electricity, but only when she was tired. She had odd, swirling dreams. Lyn did wonder if the electrical currents influenced them.

It was May when Lyn began the trip. The landscape changed slowly. The land flattened and rose. She crossed highways and farms and pastures. She forded creeks, climbed fences.

Dogs chased her. Vultures swarmed overhead. Lyn wondered if the vultures weren't used to seeing people along the path formed by the power lines.

Mice scurried underfoot.

Herds of deer cleared out ahead of Lyn. She slept in the soft nesting spots the deer made in the pastures.

She felt like a reindeer making its way to a wintering spot.

When she reached Texas, she kept going. She could walk through Central America, South America. She could walk for years.

Her legs didn't want to stop. She would walk to Patagonia, to the penguins, as far as the land would take her.

Lyn's feet hurt. Her legs ached. It didn't matter. Someone would have to shoot her: she wasn't stopping for anything less.

The Sprinter

The day after his mother's funeral the businessman wears his jogging suit to work. They know his mother died. He'll do what he wants.

The businessman's jogging suit is orange with blue racing stripes down the legs. A yellow V soars across the front when the top is zipped up. The businessman tells his secretary that he wants to be comfortable. She nods.

At eleven o'clock the flower delivery service brings the businessmen bouquets of snapdragons and roses and lilies and pink and white carnations. The businessman doesn't look up. He points to the table in the corner of his office.

His mother always hated flowers. His grandmother was a suffragette who thought flowers smacked of Victorian principles. She wouldn't eat at a restaurant that displayed even a single rose. His mother paved over their backyard, creating an expansive patio with benches. No flowers.

The businessman will give these bouquets to his secretary; let her husband deal with the stink.

Before he eats lunch, the businessman wants to burn energy. Taking the elevator down to K Street, he stretches his calves, his abdominals. As the men and women in suits make their way up and down K Street, the businessman leans into a starting position. He crouches near the mailbox. At the count of three, he sprints down the sidewalk to the newspaper box, then back. He knocks bags and packages and briefcases out of hands. One woman falls over trying to get out of his way. A UPS man cusses him out.

The businessman announces that his mother just died. He knows that will shut them up. He crouches into a starting position. The men and women in suits and heels part for him, and he bolts through the space between them, and back to the mailbox.

He knows he will go home that night, shred her pictures, her gifts, anything he owns that reminds him of his mother. He knows he will avoid talking to his sisters, to his wife, to his children. He knows this may lead to separation, divorce, something worse. But for now he likes the semblance of control. For now he is in a rhythm. He sprints. He sprints again. It would take an army to slow him down. This businessman.

IV. BLUE

Outer Circle

4:00

I'm not thinking about Thom when I stomp to the shed, unlock it, grab the spade, and hustle back to the box elder where I saw the two snakes wrangling underneath the oak leaves. I'm not thinking about Thom when I heave the shovel back and club it downwards as hard and fast as my arms will go. I'm not thinking about Thom when I slice the kingsnake in two, watching the two halves writhe—one counterclockwise, one the opposite. Thom has his life. I have mine. That's the way it goes sometimes. Union isn't the worst desire in the world.

"Satellites in orbit," I called us one night.

"Oh, ixnay on the melodrama," he said.

I hate his Pig Latin even more than the hipper-than-thou, ass-backwards Spanglish he breaks out with the Austin Grill servers. Show-off. Seven years and what do we have to show for it? Separate homes. Separate beds. No ring. No kids. I'd say my clock was ticking, but I'm not sure the hour hand works any longer. Son of a bitch.

While I'm indulging in reverie the other snake skedaddles through the weedy side of the shrub; I don't bother. I witness the final twitchings, the halved sucker bleeding into my crabgrass. Watching something else suffer for once brings me a dose of joy, something close to it. It's not a good feeling, but....

That's another thing Thom never did—never took care of the lawn as promised. "When I'm through you'll have a putting green. You can open up a mini-Golf course in your front yard." Oh, he could talk the talk. "Karen, the problem you have is he doesn't have a stake in things," Sheri said. Tell me about it. She knew I broke his balls for the past eighteen months. We were at loggerheads about his moving in.

I yank the work gloves out of my right ass pocket, slide them on, and carry the snake halves to the green plastic trashcan. Toss them in. What kind of name is Thom anyway? I mean, didn't his parents know the "h" is superfluous. They said it was a family thing, but that's exactly the kind of cutesy shit that drives me up a tree. Set Thom up for a life of slick maneuvers.

6:00

When he pulls into my driveway an hour late, he's grinning his usual boyish fucking grin. Instantly my defenses fold. There's the rub.

He lifts his gym bag onto one shoulder, cocks his head in this rakish, art-for-art's sake-Oscar-Wilde way, and he rolls his eyes, sheepishly, as if to say, "Hey, sorry, K. I'll do better next time." His voice dinks around in my head. But I want to hear the words, actually. I bob my head, lift my eyebrows, and he knows. Despite his many flaws, Thom is no dummy.

His tongue clicks in his mouth metallically, and he snorts.

"Hey, sorry, K. Promise I'll do better next time," he says, verbatim from my own mental script. He promises a whole lot—as if his future actions can always redeem his present failures. I resent his ability to read me, to know what I want, what I need. Thom is good with the small pleasantries, I have to say. Just not so good with the large actions—proposing, commitment, agreeing to father offspring.

I walk inside. He follows, strips off his jacket and sweaty grey t-shirt and shorts. His plate is in the oven (I've already eaten). I serve it to him with two oven mitts. For a moment I realize I'm the spitting image of winter. He's summer. No wonder we can't get on the same page. His plate features a bed of wild rice, grilled rockfish with lime and cilantro, steamed baby carrots, two stuffed mushrooms. I hand him a glass of lemonade. Sometimes I wish Tom drank more than the occasional glass of wine or bottle of beer. That would be something we could do together—get trashed, arm over arm, eyes marked XXX. His face is relaxed, at ease. From where Thom sits life is good. How does the chestnut go? Why buy the cow when you can have the milk for free?

8:00

Thom steps from the shower smelling of lilac and honey— thanks to the homemade soap Sheri gave me. Her daughter turned three the day she brought that soap over. Melanie rolled around on the living room floor that day until she grew dizzy. Thom removes the beige towel and slings it over the antique rocking chair my great aunt Gwendolyn gave me. Wednesday is our normal weekday evening together. "Hump day," he says, grinning. I admit it: Thom has an infectious smile. I want to put the screws to him right now, make him understand the importance of the steps I need to see him take pronto. I want to make his grin disappear. I want to watch him cower under the wrath of a woman scorned. But I can't help it: he's so exposed and clumsy. Still, he smells great, and I don't want to ruin the evening. I know I will kick myself later, but I can't help it. He splays one hand between my shoulder blades and his fingers press into my tension points and I can feel his bristly chest hair through my silk blouse.

10:00

We watch *Baby Face* on Ted Turner's channel. I tell Thom Barbara Stanwyck is the sexiest woman imaginable, especially considering she's not a natural beauty, per se. She pulls it off. I know it's an exaggeration, but he doesn't disagree. I laugh witnessing John Wayne playing one of Lily's boyfriends. Young and without his cowboy hat he is almost unrecognizable. We should all be so lucky.

Thom reclines on the couch. I sit straight-backed on the loveseat, fortressed by pillows. Thom drinks a beer while I pluck at the pillow upholstery.

12:00

When I sliced the snake in half I knew I wouldn't tell Thom. I knew he'd scold me, tell me it was unnecessary, that a kingsnake isn't hurting anybody, that if anything it would hunt down mice, vermin, that I shot myself in the foot. Fine, I'd keep it to myself. Let him see how it feels in the outer circle. I even feel guilty about this. I should disclose anyway. I'm the one always asking for more info, more scoops from his inner landscape. Still, I've always hated snakes. And I feel girly about it. And in the end I don't care. It's a physical revulsion. I'm human; I'm allowed.

He's already asleep, left arm thrown back behind his head as if he were striking a grand suicidal pose. His legs are askew. One foot dangles out of the covers. If the sheets and comforter aren't tucked in just so I can't sleep. I am both amused and jealous of his ease. It is effortless to be Thom. Must be. He doesn't sleep so much as collapse into unconsciousness. Then he's up seven hours later, refreshed. I am fitful.

I have promised myself not to bide my time, but in the end what's the difference really? We adore each other in this life we're given, and if our relationship was different I'd find some other flaw. Parallel universes reveal faulty logic of comparison. I'm sure I'll change my mind later. For now, I rest my hand on Thom's face and watch the slow movement of his diaphragm. I am not thinking of him when I circle his finger with my thumb and pinkie. I am not making a furtive wish. I am breathing with him and feeling flesh against flesh and sinking into the rhythm of what it is we have.

Hatchling

The coffee machine sounds like a barking dog. Through the small window the moon shimmers in the toilet bowl. Frank doesn't mind living in 800 square feet. He enjoys the feeling of condensation. The mold has grown tiresome though. The bloody phlegm. Frank pisses into the moon, then spits into the froth. He watches the piss water congeal back to moon. He leans over the water.

This night Frank paces. Tomorrow Emily will be eighteen. Upstairs Frank can hear them stomping. He can hear her on the phone with her little friends. Frank is a friend too. He has always been a friend. But she won't visit him. He has to bump into her on the way out, or chat her up on the porch, or "accidentally" open the laundry room when she moves her wet shorts and panties from washer to drier. She smiles, but stares straight ahead. She never does anything wrong, Frank thinks. She's the perfect creation. He can't imagine she ever shits. The toxins just evaporate.

When little Emily was born he had just moved in. Her parents gave him a deal. This is what friends of the family do, he thought. They had once raised the rent. This was a kind of rent control. He was happy this way. He could walk up the hill to the candy factory each morning and each evening slump back, shoulders hunched. He would offer his landlords bags of candy. When little

Emily sprouted teeth, he would offer her candy. She would thank him.

Frank's foster mother pulled his teeth one by one. She gave him a baby jar to collect the teeth, and he still has them. She gave him jars for his fingernail clippings, his toe-nail clippings. The mayonnaise jar she gave him for his semen was too small. His little foster brothers were amazed how quickly he could fill it. By the time he began working at the candy factory he had a coffee can. "You're a good kid, Franky," his foster mother said. She didn't say the right words. To Frank, she was only good for feeding him, for giving him containers.

When Frank first saw the little hatchling he could barely restrain himself. She was the most beautiful being he had ever seen. The whitest skin, the pinkest cheeks. She smelled like margarine one day, like coconut the next. His landlords would let him hold her. His landlords would let him feed her. He helped change her diapers. Frank didn't even mind the scent of her. He was their babysitter on reserve. He was in love.

Frank thought of her as the hatchling: he knew he would save himself for her. Falling in love at twenty is a blessing, he thought. He would hear the men in the candy factory talk about messy breakups, about quarrels. Frank thought about his love for little Emily as pure, as something true. He could wait eighteen years. In the old days this was common. Frank told himself this was the right thing. Put himself on reserve.

Now Frank can't help fantasizing. He paces, not able to sleep. He coughs bloody phlegm into the sink. Tomorrow he will make his move. Will he propose to her? Perhaps she would sense what was about to happen. She was a smart hatchling. Perhaps she would understand that she needed to find experience. Experience lived in the basement, among the mold and mildew.

Frank doesn't sleep all night. He has an idea of how to win her over. He will throw his own pre-party, a party just for the two of them. Husband and hatchling. Cake and a bottle of cabernet. He will make the cake himself, invite her down to his moldy fortress. Frank feels like a troll, like some kind of subterranean cave gecko, with huge eyes and claws and albino skin. Frank showers, but he still smells like moldering chicken. He wonders if the snakes he trains would eat small parts of himself. He drops a mouse into each tank. Feeding time. Frank wants to make sure his babies can watch the spectacle with a full stomach.

When he walks up the hill, the candy factory shines in the sunrise. The sun catches feldspar crystals in the granite. Frank wonders how her face will feel, how her lips will taste, how the points of her shoulders will feel under the pressure of his palms. He will tell the hatchling all his secrets. He will tell the hatchling that he has watched her nubs grow since she was born. He will tell her that he has suffered for eighteen years for her, that he has waited for her. The hatchling's eyes will well with tears, he thinks. She will beam, aglow with mutual love. She will say the words he wants to hear. He will hear the words. He won't take no for an answer.

The cake will have chocolate frosting. It will sit moist and shuddering on the table. He will coat the icing with bits of candy, pink and red and robin's egg blue—the right colors for the moment.

Pickle Man

This one is about the guy we called Pickle Man. Pickle Man showed up in January, right after the New Year. We had a lot of guys hanging around Candy's Diner on South Dunlop Street, but Pickle Man was different. For starters, Pickle Man was in our joint every morning. Every morning he ordered the pancake and egg special for two ninety nine, the cheapest breakfast in town. He always had this big-ass jar of pickles by his side. When he wasn't eating pancakes and eggs he had his fingers in the pickle jar, fishing out another one and lifting it to his mouth. He'd suck on them things. He'd just hold each one in his mouth like a big warty cigar. Pickle Man loved his pickles.

So we have lots of cats come around for the cheap food. The homeless shelter is only two blocks away, and they kick everybody out for the day. In the morning we were like the unofficial homeless shelter cafeteria. We had to establish a two-hour table policy, meaning no matter how damn cold it was outside you could only stay two hours. It was a sour gig for a woman like me. Not much of a tip, if anything. Plus, I had to kick dudes out on a regular basis. Usually I could just snap my fingers, and a cat would settle up, limp out the door, glaring back at me like I'm the one that gave him the bum luck. But some would fall right asleep at the table. Then we established a no-sleeping policy. After that a you-can't-smell-like-dead-rat-policy. Jack Straub wanted us to move out to the suburbs, and I can't say I blame him. He was owner. But as Sheila told him—"then you lose your base."

Pickle Man was different though. He kept to himself, for one. Didn't seem to know nobody, or didn't want to. Aside from the pickles, he was also thin, tidy, shaved, bathed. He wore a grey and maroon plaid dress jacket most of the times. A bit worn, but I could see it had its use. He always wore a dress hat. Wore a brown corduroy hat, like something guys would wear in 1979 to seem bohemian but still fit in with the power lunch crowd.

Mornings I usually worked the counter where some of the regulars would sit, the guys who had been around the block a few times. They "reserved seats," and everybody knew it. They were always trying to get a smoke on the sly. But I noticed Pickle Man. I watched.

This homeless shelter would only keep guys for sixty days then a guy'd have to find a new place to crash. So I knew my time with Pickle Man was limited. I asked Mr. Straub if it was okay with him if I waited the tables for a few weeks, just for a change of pace, just to keep things fresh. Mr. Straub was always up for keeping things fresh: he went along, no problem. I started waiting on Pickle Man. I started talking to Pickle Man. Thinking about him.

Now, I'm a woman who knows her limits. I can't transform nobody. A Jesus complex doesn't get you anywhere, especially in this line of work. But with Pickle Man, I just figured he had stories to tell. I like stories. If I wasn't good at listening I wouldn't be here.

It took me a few days to find his trust. Aside from the normal small talk, I gave him a little extra syrup, an extra egg. I even snuck him a fruit cup. His eyes widened. He knew that I went above and beyond the call of duty. He knew that. Pickle Man wasn't stupid. By the end of January I felt as if I could ask him a few questions here and there.

One morning Pickle Man came in and sat at the booth in back. He usually liked his privacy to read his paper, eat his pickles in peace. It was a quiet morning, warm outside so some of the guys from the shelter were basking in the sun. I thought of seals or penguins. This was a Baltimore winter we're talking about, not South Florida. So I asked him if I could sit down next to him, take a load off. He rotated his fork in one hand in and out of his fingers. He didn't say anything so I just sat. He was done with his pancakes and eggs. His water glass was still full. I could hear him unscrewing his pickle jar with his other hand. He brought a small round pickle to his mouth, and he sank his teeth into it. I watched a small green jet of pickle juice shoot onto the floor.

"So you really like those things, huh?" I tried to not sound sarcastic. I didn't want to scare him off. Just couldn't help myself. I listened for the bell at the door. If I heard that I'd have to go and seat the new customers. Since I believed in luck (still do), I crossed my fingers.

"Yeah," he said. I could hear him screwing the pickle jar closed.

"Don't you ever get sick of pickles?" I didn't want to go too fast. If I kept the conversation at the surface level, I was bound to win him over. This is what I told myself. He shoved the rest of the pickle in his mouth and swallowed. He chewed with his mouth open. I was willing to overlook this.

"No," he said. "Not really." He stared at the empty chairs across the aisle from him. He bored a hole into the wall. He didn't look up at the customers sitting at the breakfast bar. He didn't look out the window, or out the door.

"So why do you think you like the taste of them so much?" I asked. I felt as if I was talking to a child—this was what my job came down to sometimes. New strategies. Taking life at a new glance.

When I watched Pickle Man's reaction I could tell the question hit a nerve. This is when things changed really quick. He dropped his fork on the floor and squinted and furrowed his brow as if he'd never heard this question before, as if this was some kind of Eureka moment. I thought right then and there he was about to relate his life story to me, to tell me how he got so scarred. Instead, he stood up. He kicked the fork across the dining room to the men sitting at the counter, and then he turned to me.

"You ask *them* about that," he said, pointing to where he kicked the fork. He walked up to the register, carrying his pickle jar in both arms. One of the men at the counter stifled a laugh, and then as Pickle Man walked by they all started cracking up.

"I think you lost something, Pickle Man!" one of them said, pointing to the fork.

"You like the shape of them pickles, Pickle Man?" another said. "Look like nasty green cocks you ask me." They laughed it up.

"Guess you don't need no fork to eat them nasty-assed pickles," another one said.

I was still sitting there at the booth, watching him go.

For another week I didn't have the guts to approach him. I just didn't want to annoy him, to get him worked up. Didn't want to make life more difficult for him than it already was, so I did as he said and I asked the regulars at the counter. Most of them just laughed me off, but when things settled down, Harvey leaned toward me and whispered.

"Here's your Pickle Man's story," he said. "He was a fancy

lawyer. Had a wife. A house. Everything. But the man worked his ass off. He was up in his office eighty, ninety, one hundred hours a day. Seven days a week." Harvey took an illicit drag off his cigarette and held it down by his thigh where nobody could see it, especially Straub. "Nearly killed hisself. Had a near heart attack working so much. Just overloaded the system, know what I mean? After he recovered, he quit. He took off out of here. He wandered around, like all the air came out of the balloon. His wife filed for a divorce. Sold the house. Poof. Something snapped in the man."

That afternoon I trudged over to the homeless shelter and did some more nosing around. Calvin, who manned the desk, wasn't supposed to spill personal beans, but he said it has become common knowledge that Pickle Man used to live right down the road on Lovelace Ave in one of those big old blue stone houses that look like castles. The guy has never gotten over the loss, Calvin said. Felt exiled or something, I thought. Pickle Man walked by his old house every day, Calvin told me. Used to before he stayed at the shelter. "He'd sleep in the park across the street, until some of his old neighbors began housing him," Calvin said. "When they couldn't do anything for him anymore, he came here." All that money, all that work, I thought—what a waste.

When I got back home that night I couldn't get Pickle Man off my mind. I poured myself a stiff drink and turned up the boob tube as loud as it gets to drown out the thoughts whirring in my head. I knew I was getting over an ex myself. I couldn't plug up every hole of suffering. I could only do so much. I poured myself another drink. Then another. Zapped myself some leftovers in the microwave. Curled up with my cats. Fell asleep in front of the television.

The next day Pickle Man was gone. Checked out last night,

Calvin said. Nobody seen him since. Him or his jar of pickles. All that week I couldn't sleep. I started dreaming about Pickle Man. Nothing sexual really, just snuggling, cuddling. But he was there in my bed, on my sofa, on my floor. Him and his salty pickles. In one dream Pickle Man told me he liked pickles because they reminded him of lunch. When he was a lawyer he'd go to this deli for lunch. It was the only break he took from seven in the morning until nine at night. And he loved pickles. The sandwiches were good, but the pickles were the best he ever had. Then the deli closed. He always took that as a sign.

I didn't see Pickle Man all spring. But in the summer I was walking with my niece at sunset in the park down by the river, and there he was about a football field away. He was sitting on a bench. He looked so different though. He was wearing an all-white jumpsuit, a white headband. Like one of those old pictures of Jimmy Connors or something. Pickle Man's shoes were so white it was difficult to look at them. He was holding a tennis racquet with a wooden frame. I bet Pickle Man used to play tennis every night. I leaned over to my niece and told her that the man sitting on the bench is Pickle Man. She knew all about him.

"We have to hurry," I said. "Don't know where he's staying." I looked down at my watch to see what time it is, and when I looked up I didn't see him. He wasn't there on the bench. He wasn't walking around. I ran over to where I saw him, but he just wasn't there.

I closed my eyes and smelled the balmy air. I could hear the gentle flow of the river. I could see him there glowing in the light of his own private court, practicing his serve. The yellow-green ball arcing up, dropping, the racquet swiveling forward, and then thunk. The jar of pickles was there in the pantry, where it was supposed to be.

Away

When Marcus calls, I answer, even if it is three in the morning. This month he's in Jakarta and Singapore. Manila and Taipei. Bangkok and Rangoon. The time difference is too confusing for him, I'm sure. It is for me. The important part: He sounds glad to hear my voice. When Marcus calls I never tell him I miss his company. That may give him the impression that I worry, or that I'm lonely after six weeks of his absence. Six weeks—that's nothing. I live my life. I'm fine. No cracks in the edifice.

Marcus sounds upbeat on the phone this time, a joyful clatter behind him, soft tinny music barely audible. I can almost feel the sway of grass huts, the umbrellas, the tropical breezes. He tells me he's in a restaurant and that yesterday he had a chance to see the most amazing sites. He recounts names and places, but they just wash over me. I tell him I'm *delighted* for him, that I'm glad to hear he's having a wonderful time. "Well, here's my bill," Marcus tells me. He says he has to run. More important business transactions, more conferences, he says. More wheeling, dealing. I remove my glasses and rub my eyes. I can feel the indentations on my nose. They feel like craters.

I know, of course. When he returns from his trips, I can see the boredom in his posture. He brings gifts, which I add to our show-me cabinet filled with vases and bowls and trinkets and hand-engraved wood from all over the world. I want to sit him down, tell him what I was thinking while he was away. I want a discussion. But this is not meant to be or it would happen. Marcus is awfully busy.

I do know what he does out there. He hasn't told me, and I don't have any physical proof, but I still know. His smile is cracked and diffused in prism-like refractions. In the recesses of his eyes I can see the others.

The reality is I am musty and old, too thick, trunk-like. To him I must look like a prudish old biddy. I must seem asexual. Something has to change.

I made an appointment at the mall. The doctor said it was only two grand per eye, and I thought it sounded like a steal. Since I was sixteen I've worn glasses. For a small fee Marcus can view me in the way he once did. He can see my face for what it is—stripped clean of obstacles.

This will be a surprise to him. When Marcus returns in a week it will be done. The new period in our life can then begin. In two years I can afford to retire, and then I can hitch myself to him, join him in Buenos Aires and Sao Paulo. Lima and Quito. Then *he* will have to adjust. Perhaps then I will unlearn what I have already learned. Perhaps then I will see the sights in carmine and terra cotta, in verdigris and cornflower blue. I will descend.

Joyce

Smiles as if she's about to ask me a profane question, something nasty, something that will throw me off-guard.

I don't care. Let her.

Let Joyce do as she wants. She will anyway. I've tried to break down her defenses, but her defenses aren't even defenses. They're mirrors leading to more mirrors.

She's wearing pancake makeup today, covering up her blemishes, her acne. She's always had gnarly skin. Self-conscious.

She's wearing twin hoop earrings, each one adorned with three white pearls, all in a row. Something about this reminds me of the abacus.

Her hair always looks sweaty, pasted to her brow, pasted to the wedge of skin in front of her ears.

She's not beautiful, yet she's captivating anyway in her own way.

Those eyes—the size of half-dollars, the darkest brown, dark as her hair. The trio of faint freckles by her mouth—right side, then two on each side of the cleft.

As for her sweater, the vertical lines that go from her neck straight down are there just to fuck with me.

Joyce likes fucking with me. It makes her feel better about

her lot in life.

She likes ending our phone conversations on her terms—*when* she wants to, why she wants to.

Today she enjoys undermining my achievements.

But if I said this she'd laugh me off, tell me to quit being "morose." We sit in a coffee shop, clattering on our respective laptops, breathing burnt coffee beans together. We do this a lot. We look at each other. Joyce twirls her hair, licks her teeth clean.

My wife can't stand Joyce, but then there must be some part of her that knows.

A repressed sliver.

I can't help myself: I'm transfixed. Come pain, come suffering. When she turns away, my breath goes as well.

Why does difficulty inspire passion? It shouldn't be that way.

"I'm not *difficult*," Joyce says. "I'm simple."

As simple as a knife through the ribs, I think. Simpler.

When my wife turns into an ex I'll miss these times. For now they are a brand of pale poison.

Respect the Process

Ed says. Ed would know. "Don't force it." I've got the back end.

"Yeah, yeah," I say. Ed's onea those guys, likes to dole out advice, massage his own ego. I'll listen because I have to. He's my boss when it comes to deliveries. I'm moonlighting—if you can moonlight on Sunday afternoons. Anyway, that's what I do instead of going to church or watching football.

"Go ahead," he says. "I got it. It's not a heavy piece. It's a children's bureau. We're parked in front of a little rambler, can't be any more than two thousand square feet, even with a basement.

I back down the ramp, boot treads on steel treads. Then we're up the driveway, sidewalk, up the stairs, down the hall, into the kid's room. Boom, up against the wall. Piecea cake.

We have five more deliveries to make and I look at my watch. Three thirty already. No way we'll be done by five, and who wants a furniture delivery interrupting their Sunday family supper. If I had a family supper I wouldn't, but that's my mistake. God, I do miss it sometimes... the simple things most of all. Ed says I'm making myself suffer, penance or some shit. Lifting, moving, these are just things to fill time. I go nuts staying at home, gets me into hot water.

"There's a downside to remembering," Ed told me once. He's right about that.

"As we're walking out the woman asks, "Hey, you two, would you like to see something interesting?"

This could go in a thousand directions, I think, most of them leading to trouble. Ed eyeballs me, slides his lower lip over his upper. I shrug.

"Sure," he says. "But we have a busy schedule."

"That's okay," she says. "It'll only take a second."

She points one twisted finger at us and eggs us on back upstairs past the kids' room into the master suite. As far as we know it's just us three there. No husband or kids around. This concerns me. The woman has a lazy right eye and tinted glasses to boot, orangey hair. She seems a screw or two off.

Clicking the bedroom door closed, the woman immediately lifts her shirt, lifts her bra. Underneath is one beautiful tit, and in the place where the other was there's a flat plane, a raised score.

"Mastectomy," she says. "But I kicked it. How about that? 100% healthy now."

I look at it, then look off. The room is painted blue and a large fish tank is mounted above the bed. I watch the fins slice through the light.

"I'm sorry," I say. I mean it. I'm not sure what else to say. "I didn't know."

"Don't be," she says. "I'm not. Just thought you might like to see a close call." She knocks on the place where her tit used to be.

"It's amazing," Ed says. His face is drawn back. He reminds me of a horse in concentration. He's transformed. Her shirt is still up.

"Can we touch it?"

"Oh sure," she says. "I don't care."

Ed and me, we press our hands to the flatness. We take turns and then my hand and his press around. The woman laughs, kicks her head back. I can see the caps on her cavities. The fins slice through the shifting light. Her breathing slows a bit and so does ours. Then we're done. We all are.

The Thermos

The hills actually do roll, Shep Forston thought. He squinted through the bug-smeared window and out toward the hills and vales, what was left of the undeveloped land. The trees and brush and prairies gave way to crests, capped by ancient knotted oaks that seemed to sag from the weight of their own branches. Red maples and pines and elms angled down the hills. Then houses: miles and miles of houses, the land stripped as flat and bare as the sky. The limbs of young pear trees shuffled in the wind—an insult to injury, Shep thought.

"Can I have 'nother piece?" Shep asked, pointing to the gum. Benjy snorted and blew his nose into his fingers. Then he worked his fingers into his jeans. A fine mist descended and Benjy hit the wipers. It almost looks fake, Shep thought. Shep didn't know if the snort meant yes or no, but with Benjy it didn't rightly matter. Shep would do what he wanted anyway. He snapped a piece from the package and held the nub of the gum between his index finger and thumb.

"How much longer?" Shep asked.

"Ten, maybe fifteen miles," Benjy said. "You got a bus to catch?"

"That's good," Shep said. "You're doing a good job."

People told Shep that he had a soft side, always checking up on people. Maternal almost. He didn't see it that way, and regardless he didn't appreciate being referred to as womanly. Shep didn't mind giving positive feeling, that's all. What does that have to do with being a woman?

Shep held the Thermos between his knees and flicked the gum wrapper open. He could feel the warmth radiating from inside, the corn chowder his mother made. That and the saltines in his pocket and he would be good to go until dark. Benjy said no guarantees, but Shep knew he did well face to face. On the phone forget it, but give him a day to impress and Shep knew he would come through.

"What's the namea this guy again?" Shep asked.

"Julius Carlton," Benjy said. "Told you already."

"Julius? Like Dr. J?"

"Who?"

"You're kidding me. You know. Basketball player," Shep said. "Way back when."

"What the hell do I care 'bout basketball?" Benjy said.

"Just makin' conversation," Shep said.

"Yeah, well, make it about something I've heard of. Least you can do."

Shep popped the new gum in his mouth, chewing it into his flavorless older piece. Ever since he gave up smoking he had to have something in his mouth. Gum was better than the other options. He was ready to tackle drinking next, a tougher task. Shep wanted to clean himself out entirely. Then exercise. Working out once a day, everyday. Stay active. Shep wanted a regimen, something to set him straight.

Benjy hit the gas and took a sharp right onto Glenwood Drive. Benjy's truck mounted the hill and climbed it, and rolled down the rear of the hill. Shep could smell the exhaust. When he was a kid he actually liked the smell—it was adult; it reminded him of money, of work, of men taking the world by the horns. Gasoline was the smell of adulthood. When Shep turned forty that changed, everything did. When his father died and he moved back home, Shep knew he wouldn't move again until the other shoe dropped. If he ever wanted to get out of Dodge it would have to wait. His mother came first.

"Hey, Benjy," Shep said. "'Member that tile job we did down by the reservoir?"

"Which one?"

"You know, the one with the crazy old lady. She came onto me and all. That one."

Benjy said the woman *never* came onto Shep, ever, not on his watch. Benjy said as long as H&H Handyman is in existence we're going to be professional. We've always been and always will be professional. It's time to turn a new leaf; enough of this shit, he said.

"You can't go into this job chowing down like that," Benjy said. He wiped his hand on his pants again. "Like a damn swine."

"Why not? All we're doing is—"

"Representing the company," Benjy said. "I know. That's what we're doing. I mean, look we have to have a clean image or we ain't getting more work, hear? Any complaints and we're both out of a job."

Shep wondered what kind of job is a job that don't pay. H&H must be the worst run company in the county, Shep thought. When they do get a project, it only lasts a day or two, and then they'll go for weeks without nothing. If it weren't for the insurance money he'd be up shit's creek. He might be anyway, he thought.

Shep spat the gum into the leftover wrapper and pocketed it

for later use. He didn't know how Benjy got so bossy. He's not even the boss, Shep thought. All he does is drive. Sometimes Shep wondered if Benjy took advantage of him. The fact that Shep lived at home with his mother shouldn't have anything to do with anything. He couldn't help certain things, could he?

In the not-so-distant past Shep's family worked the land; Shep heard all the stories about the good old days. The land was everything back then. Shep wondered where all the people were who used to own this county—the Hinkles, the Pinkertons, the Gurneys.... Where were all of them now? Too bad them Forstons sold all their farmland thirty years ago, Shep thought. Otherwise, he'd be rich. He would've grown corn and potatoes and squash and beans and live off the bounty of the soil. And he wouldn't sell his land to developers or lease it out to other farmers who would tear it up and poison the soil. Shep would value what he had and the good life he could live on it. Life would have been different, better.

That day and into the next Shep and Benjy laid drywall in the Carlton's basement. It was a simple job. Shep could have done that one in his sleep by himself. When they finished they didn't receive another job for weeks. Sometimes when they were desperate Benjy would take Shep down to the 7-Eleven early in the morning where the Honduran day laborers gathered. Sometimes Shep and Benjy would work the orchards for three dollars an hour with the Hondurans, just to get out of the house, to feel productive. Other times they would pick spinach and greens on farms two counties west. It was backbreaking work, but at least it was something.

Otherwise Shep spent most of his time taking care of his mother, going shopping for her, helping her around the house, helping her with money. If they were rich Shep would hire a nice college student to help his mother with these things. The insurance money only went so far. Sometimes his mother wore him down. Ever since Pop died she was so needy, so reliant. Shep didn't know how his mother would survive without him. His mother could cook and clean, but that was about it.

After his mother went to sleep at night Shep would sit in the kitchen smelling the residue of past dinners soaked into the walls: beef and barley, sweet potatoes, onions. He would sit at the kitchen table and imagine his father sitting across from him at the head of the table, hunching forward over a cup of coffee and toast, his hands shaking from the caffeine. Shep would picture his sister next to him, leaning into her dinner plate, lifting her head at the slightest mumble or cough. Shep wished she didn't live all the way on the other side of the country. He could use a family hand.

As he washed out his Thermos, Shep would stare out into the night. Even on the days he didn't work Shep would still drink from the same old Thermos. He loved the ugly rust-brown color of it, the way it made him feel like a hunter in an old 70's movie or something. It reminded Shep of simpler times. Whatever he put inside it was always perfectly cold or perfectly hot or it seemed so. It was as if the Thermos knew, as if it had a premonition. The Thermos wasn't exactly a lucky possession, but it was something like that. Even his vodka and grape juice tasted better coming from the Thermos.

Shep always wondered what would have happened if he went to college. Like his sister did. The two years Shep lived on his own were so strange. He would constantly drive home to eat his mother's food, to do his laundry in the old house. But an apartment wasn't hope, Shep thought. Still... his life would have been different. Once, Benjy told Shep he needed to stop being a mama's boy. Someday maybe that would come true; Shep could only hope one day his duties lifted.

"She needs me around," Shep said.

"But what do *you* need?" Benjy asked him once. "You're an adult, ain't you?" Shep wished Benjy had his problems. Then and only then would he understand.

Shep ran his finger around the ridged Thermos cap. He didn't feel like answering the question exactly. But then again he would rather keep things as simple as possible. The warmth from the Thermos was good. He had something to look forward to. He could focus on that for the time being.

Whipped

When Abe told us he found his soulmate, we were ecstatic. For years we had watched him mope, complaining that it was so difficult to meet cute, young, open-minded, free-spirited women here. "This town is too *uptight*, too stuffy," he moaned. What he really wanted was a granola girl, a hippie chick who shared his hippie man values. We thought Abe was setting his sights too narrowly, that he was confining his choices, restricting his view on life. Plus, Abe was shy, always tentative, awkward, and ungainly. In his own way he was a catch, but we hoped the person he was looking for actually still existed in the twenty first century in the shape and form he hoped she would. He had this Platonic ideal.

Then Abe met Melissa, and claimed he had finally found bliss. Of course we wanted to meet her right away. We wanted to see this so-called "bliss." But as Abe said, he wanted some time to *develop* with Melissa before social pressures set in: Abe said he wanted to make sure first. Abe said he didn't want to rush, to seem too eager. He said we could wait a week, maybe two, maybe three.

When we met Melissa we couldn't have been more disappointed. Abe said she was a "real cutie," that she was "kind and big-hearted." He said Melissa was "passionate." Sadly, we didn't see evidence of any these qualities. Melissa seemed scrawny and her face was scored with acne pits. She bore a stunned squinty look as if she were a naked mole rat crawling from its burrows. She had mean little nubs for eyes. Rather than passion we saw a control freak bent on cold calculation. Instead of kindness we saw contemptuous manipulation. Abe has always been soft, but we suspected Melissa wanted a man she could push around. Abe was perfect for this.

Of course we couldn't mention our theories or insights to Abe.

At any rate, Abe was off on his usual circuit—skateboarding, surfing, lighting up joints on his balcony while listening to Rusted Root. We joined him, feigning interest. When we asked about Melissa, Abe grinned. We sighed. We threw up our hands. Abe was so tall and muscular, so kind, so graced with an easy nature. Melissa didn't *deserve* him. Despite his goofiness, his floppy hair and baseball caps, Abe was a man with whom many a woman would be content. Not that we are superficial or in the least bit judgmental. Our overtures to Melissa on this subject were acknowledged with only a shrug. We tried.

To our increasing dismay, months and years passed and Abe still remained with Melissa. Though she began as a librarian she metamorphosed into a telemarketer. From books to hooks. Melissa began acquiring jewelry and furs. Abe shook these trends off as temporary, and said that a little materialism was absolutely normal. "We all have to have some things," he said. "She still has a pure heart."

Melissa became snippy, then downright nasty. She called Abe "chubby bubby," ordering him to lose weight or else. She told Abe he had to stop wasting his life. She told him to "get a job, a real job, a job with *teeth*." Melissa said he needed to "stop wearing homeless man rags," to start "acting like a grown man." When we attempted to come to his rescue, Melissa told us to "butt the hell out," then said Abe wouldn't be seeing us "ne'er-do-wells" any time soon. He detailed the ways and means by which she would sic the heat upon us if we even ventured near her abode.

This was his dream woman?

While Melissa made some strong points, her "truths" were crusted over with untruths and exaggerations. We discussed options for her removal. We made voodoo dolls. We offered prayers. We began noticing bruises on Abe's face, Band-Aids on his shoulders, slashes on his neck and hands. Abe said it was nothing at all. He shook the wounds off as some "surfing scrapes and things, I don't know." We wondered.

When we asked Abe once why he was with Melissa he said, "I didn't think I would find another woman; women don't think I'm interesting." We scratched our heads. We told him we like him. "That's a start," he said. "But I have to branch out." We could see the crack in the edifice. Abe walked, watching his shoes. He scuffed along.

But then Melissa moved in with Abe, telling him that the walls had to be yellow, that they had to buy ornate handmade Kazakhi rugs. Obscure and exotic. Abe began paying two thirds of the rent. This was his "punishment" for not holding a job. Melissa said this would give Abe incentive. Abe began doing all the cooking, all the cleaning. "What else do you have to do?" Melissa asked. She began wearing muddy shoes around the house, just so Abe would have to clean up after her. Even though we weren't invited, we watched.

When Melissa began whipping Abe with a bamboo stick, we had to intervene. Abe didn't say a word. He hung his head, stared at the floor. We made him sleep on our sofa, and we told him he wasn't allowed outside until Melissa was gone. He didn't complain. "I guess you're right," he said. "For some reason we're not working. I guess it's just not..." He looked off into the distance.

By the time we made it to Abe's old house, she had packed her bags. Her car was gone. The furniture was gone. She left behind pictures though, the pictures she took of the two of them scattered on the floor. We couldn't help but look. In many of the pictures Abe was smiling, vacant and as distant as if he were a tourist in front of Mt. Rushmore. In others, Abe was contorted into odd and embarrassing positions. In some he held tennis balls or bananas in his mouth, like a show monkey. We could just about hear echoes of Melissa's screechy voice ordering Abe around. Do this. Do that. Hold still.

For months Abe slept on our guest bed, unable to return to his home. We didn't hurry him at all. We put him to work in the yard digging holes and trimming weeds, whatever we could find. When we had nothing better to do we would kick Abe, bite his ears to wake him up in the morning.

"Hurry up you lazy idiot," we'd say. "What do you think, this is your home? Let's go!"

Huzun

My name is Tom Small. In high school my friends would give me a hard time about that: I'm 6'7", two fifty-six. And no, I never played basketball. Hate that question.

I work for VDOT. Toll booth operator at the intersection of the Dulles Toll Road and Route Seven. Correct: you really cannot imagine a duller, more rote job. I make change for a living. That's the whole of it, really. When I'm not making change I'm sitting there, watching the minutes go by. Minutes, hours, days, seasons, years. Every day is about the same as the one before and after it. I arrive at nine in the evening and leave and five in the morning. I unwind from five thirty to seven thirty, then sleep from seven thirty to about three. Clockwork.

About a year ago we hired Melek. May. Melek was a sixteen-year-old kid. Parents are from Turkey, though she was born here. Speaks good English. Didn't have to take ESL classes or anything. We don't have a tremendous amount of time for socialization when we're in the box, so it took a while to get to know her. Still, during changeovers we'd talk—Melek worked an abbreviated shift from three to seven.

Every weekday we'd chat for about ten, fifteen minutes—school, family, TV shows. Chitchat. I enjoyed it—began arriving early just to catch her. Oddly, she was a glum girl—hardly ever smiled. It didn't help that she wore dark eye shadow, which gave her the appearance of a meerkat.

One day we were in the "transition room," when I called her on her smile—or lack thereof.

"Smiling is so *American*," she said. "Why do I need to smile all the time? I don't always have something to smile about."

"That's honest," I said. "I'll give you that."

"Do you know about huzun?" she asked. Melek squinted at me with her large green eyes. Her head was small, features fine. Cute, I'll admit it. I shook my head, partially at her question, partially at the twenty-three tragic years that separated us.

"It's this thing in Turkey—other countries too. You believe you're cursed, basically. Sad all the time, missing what we used to be. It's hard to explain. Hard to translate accurately. Nostalgia maybe."

"So you're blaming your culture for not smiling now?" I admit, I was flirting. Can't throw me in the clink for that.

"No, no, I'm just saying…"

Melek rubbed at her temples, said she had a migraine. I didn't think anything of it. I offered her an Advil, but she said they don't help. I thought she just wanted to end the conversation—perfectly understandable, I thought at the time.

"I'm going home," she said. "My mother needs me."

Weeks and months passed. The weather became hot and humid, a green haze hanging over everything. It didn't change much of what I did in the box. The only tough part was keeping cool—all that heat from the exhaust, the heat rising from the asphalt. Otherwise, I tried to keep my booth clean, swept. I imagined it as a second home, something to take care of. I tried to wave to the drivers, say "hi," and "thank you." I tried to keep the line moving as fast as possible. The simple things.

Melek began missing a day here and there. We'd still chat from 7:00 to 7:15 each weekday, and I missed that part of my routine when she wasn't at work—but something was wrong. I knew that.

I got Melek's home number when our supervisor (Mitch) stepped out for a cigarette break. I called from my "prohibited" cell one balmy July evening. The moths lollygagged around the sodium lamps.

"Hello," the voice said. "Who this?"

"This is Tom," I said. "I work with Melek."

"Melek?" The voice said. Had to be her mother. "Melek sick. She call you."

Then she hung up. I don't know, maybe Melek's mother didn't want her to have male friends.

The next morning (Saturday), my cell phone goes haywire. "Knock, knock, knocking on heaven's door" ring tone. Guilty pleasure. I'm asleep, but I pick up—thinking, maybe unconsciously, that it might be Melek. I wanted to help. Maybe I felt paternal on some level.

"This is Melek," she announced, as if I just called her.

"Yes…hi, Melek," I said. "How are you *feeling*?"

"I'm in the hospital right now," she said.

I sat up. "Oh my God, what happened?"

"Just testing. They are always testing. You didn't know that?"

"Know what?"

She told me she was diagnosed with lupus and three other diseases I had never heard of. She had to go to the specialists regularly, just so they could monitor her progress. It was her version of normal.

"I just didn't want you to worry. Thank you for calling me to check in," she said. "I'm fine. I'm not depressed."

This last bit got me thinking, honestly. It definitely fell into the lady doth protest too much category, for starters. I know she probably *was* depressed, but figured that was a result of her multiple illnesses.

Then Melek returned to work.

She looked pale, gaunt, her skin desiccated. When she saw me Melek tried to smile. It was painful to watch. Then I realized I could be projecting—making Melek's 16-year old life into some cheesy after-school special.

Melek sat at one of the picnic tables in the break room. She puffed her hair from her eyes—it drooped back, dangling in front of her. She let it.

"I think my mother actually *likes* being in a hospital. It's like her whole body relaxes. She stops barking at me for a few minutes. It's something to behold, really"

I expressed routine sympathy at this point.

"You're sweet," she said. Then she closed her eyes entirely. "My mother is almost *happy* when I go to see a doctor. Even better if I have to get a shot or something."

"I don't think that's likely."

"No, it's true," she said. "It is." Melek reiterated that her mother has been giving shots all her life. "She'd always smile then," Melek said. "Maybe that's why I don't."

This sent chills up my arms—a mother elated by her child's illness. I didn't get it. Seemed impossible, I thought, but then my mother was always good to me.

"What about your father?"

"She divorced him. She said he cheated her out of money so she sued him, straight up. It was very bad. So he's not around anymore."

When I went home I began searching around the Internet for any information on parents taking delight in their own children's physical maladies. I found plenty. More than plenty. Parents—mothers mostly—injecting their sons with urine, putting nail polish into their daughter's feeding tubs, scrubbing their children with oven cleaner. Munchausen by proxy it's called. Mothers like their children to have attention, if it can be called attention." Like to incapacitate them is more like it. Always in the hospital. Calm, cool, collected, trying to get the best care for their children.

I asked Melek about this. She said one of her friends told her about this also. Long time ago.

"No, no, no," Melek said. "No, my mother loves me very much. No, she wouldn't hurt me on purpose. She loves me *too* much."

She had a bag of pistachios. She cracked each one open, one by one. Her small fingers pressed and lifted each green nut, bringing them to her lips. She ate them quickly, reminding me of a sea otter, for some reason. She looked at her hands as she did this, told me about a boy who has a crush on her. An "All-American Boy," she called him.

"He thinks I'm exotic, or something. Maybe he thinks I'm part of a harem or something. I don't know."

Melek told me she jokes with him, that she tells him she wears a veil at home (she used a different word), that her house is cloaked in silk prints and Persian rugs. They have biology class together—lab partners. All-American boy has spiky hair, she said, and he's always touching it—patting it down. One day he asked her to touch it. She looked around first, then she did.

"His hair felt like porcupine, you know. It would *hurt* me."

I told her she should give him a chance, but she continued eating her pistachios with her little otter fingers, not smiling.

Her arms looked veiny, I thought, but her eyes looked warm. I had to go to work, make change.

In 12006 I wanted a break—an early midlife respite. I had enough money saved, so I sub-letted my apartment, moved down to Myrtle Beach for a year. I got a job for thirty hours a week, working as a clerk at a seaside tourist shop. We had shells, little plastic buckets, sunscreen, T-shirts, saltwater taffy. It was an easy job, and it allowed me to essentially break even down there. Still.

I lived within walking distance to the beach, but too far away to see the ocean, or hear the thrum of waves. Every night I would sit on the deck of my apartment and feel the sea breeze. I would eat my dinners out there—takeout mostly. Sometimes I'd just boil an ear of corn and bake a potato. I didn't need much.

I took the year to reflect. I didn't *accomplish* anything. But it was the best year of my life—just me and my thoughts.

I saw on the news one night that in the middle of the Black Sea a ship stocked with twenty thousand sheep collided with another ship. The ships were near shore when this occurred, but the sheep-bearing ship began to sink, its hull ruptured. Nothing could be done about the sheep. Despite the fact that sheep can't swim, several dozen managed to jump ship and paddle to the shore. They survived. The other sheep drown. The ship's crew all managed to scramble in a life boat and make its way to shore.

When I walked to the ocean itself I thought of the bleating of thousands of sheep. I would look out over the water and think about that. I still do.

Though I wanted to ask Melek for a chance to meet her mother I realized this was an impossibility. What occasion would allow for this? My only hope was that one day Melek's mother would pick her up from work, but since Melek already owned a car (copper Celica) this didn't seem likely.

By the fall, Melek had to take three weeks off to recover from what she called "spots." I wasn't sure what that meant, but I was suspicious. I imagined her mother scrubbing her down with oven cleaner. During this time I did call several times, but I only got the machine. In the box I felt preoccupied with worry, protective. I had nightmares—garra rufa nibbling on Melek's rotting skin, her rigid cadaver sliding down an ice floe.

One night I was in the box, as usual. It was quiet enough; I could flip through a magazine. A car came through every forty five seconds or so, sometimes longer.

I looked up and saw Melek's Celica. Melik was splayed prostrate in the passenger seat, a salmon-hued blanket up to her chin. An older woman—her mother? It had to be—sat behind the wheel.

"Hi," I said. Melek waved at me. The older woman handed me a crisp one dollar bill. I already had a quarter in my hand, as usual, but I reached into the drawer for another—stalling.

"Are you Melek's mother?" I asked, only a quick glance at her. I noticed Melek had a twelve by twelve photo of her mother taped to her dashboard. Don't know if that was her mother's doing or Melek's.

"Yes, I am," she said. Her face was nearly expressionless. I noticed her hair was drawn back, tied with a small, green bow.

"Is Melek feeling better now?"

I held the quarter out to her, but didn't yet drop it in her hand. I wanted a response.

Melek's mother looked at her daughter, smoothed back her hair, touching her. Then she turned back to me.

"You work with my daughter. She tells me she like it here," her mother said. Then she withdrew a small red tube of lipstick from somewhere underneath. She applied the lipstick, watching my reaction.

"That's good," I said. And we like having her. It's—"

"Personally," her mother continued, "I don't see why."

She pressed on the gas. The Celica lurched forward. I held the quarter there, dangling in the air.

By December Melek had stopped working as a tollbooth operator, citing health problems. I would give her a call now and then, always getting the machine, always leaving a message.

I didn't forget about Melek, but the persistence of the every day was enough to dilute my memory of her. I'd think about her from time to time, but for the most part she became a diaphanous vision—sickly, wan, and peevish. Melek became an image in my mind rather than a person.

I didn't expect to read her obituary in the newspaper, and I didn't. Instead, my imagination took over. I pictured the worst, though as far as I know it never came true. I worried.

I still leave an occasional phone message, just to let her know I'm thinking of her. I haven't received a reply.

As for her mother, I've only mailed three letters—and they weren't even full threats. "Warnings" is a better word. No return address. I'm sure if I was smart enough I could think of an even better one. This will do for now. And who is to say if I'm done? I can't.

V.

NOW

and THEN

Let's Do Thai

I hear what they say when I fly close to them. He says he's sorry a lot and she nods with that quick smile. She says it's not really a smile. It's more like a frown that's laughing.

She's saying this is no way to start a weekend, and she's saying he's getting more baldy with each woman, and she's saying he is only interested in green. I thought his favorite color was red, white, and blue. That's what he said last week. I'm flying off then. Around and around. I can hear ice cubes and tink-a-tink-tink. My brother is too much of a baby, so he can't.

My arms are out to my ears, and things look small down below me. The people at the other tables laugh, and smile real smiles, and I lift my head and smile at the ceiling. I'm flying so the air feels good.

Ryan isn't really doing anything. He's eating his spaghetti-with-the-weird-name. That's what I call it. My father says he likes that. My mother shakes her head and tries to tell me the real name. Her mouth looks like one of those tropical fish. But I forget it. It's because it has grass in it and other stuff that I've never even heard of. I say I don't eat grass. I'm not a moo cow.

The guy at the door nods to me. He moves so I can fly. This is good because I need room to fly. I can fly upside down and backwards. Sideways too. Around in circles and back. Then when I'm flying back for more Coke the lady hits my head with the flat circle she's carrying with stuff on it. Things rattle and someone says be careful. Careful. Careful. Eat your food, she says. I shake my head.

I'm back and he says he doesn't like it himself. It's all everybody talks about, he says. Trendy, trendy, he says. It's all a big guilt trip, he says.

I fly to the bathroom saying trendy, trendy, trendy. I pee on the floor and fly back and forth. Yellow lines. Yellow lines. Like yellow string or that squash she likes. I don't even wash 'cause who's going to make me wash when they're not here? Plah. Plah. I wipe my hands on the sink and my shirt and I fly back. My hands don't smell like pee. They smell like skin.

He says one of us is worth ten or eleven of them. He doesn't care what she says. If they're so great why are they bringing us the food? He says they should tuck their tails between their legs and go back where they're from. We're at war anyway. His hands are balls. Her hands pick at her neck. She wipes her blood with a napkin. She dips the napkin in her glass and lifts it again. I didn't know people have tails.

She says go ahead and tell the waiter then. See how he likes it. He calls out to him, but he doesn't hear. He snaps. Then he closes one eye and walks over.

This time I fly all the way out. The doors swing behind me. I like sticking my fingers on them to see where I was. It's like sidewalks only easier.

Then I fly out to the ramp and climb on the bar things. I stand on them and jump off them and fly to the other side of the square and look in. The sky is dark and flashes are flashing. The wind is blowing. I can hear the grumbly-grumbly. The air smells and

I can hear dogs barking. Cats meowing. Cars honking.

He stands up and shoves the man. I can hear him from there. Ryan crawls under the table and she's tugging at his shirt and he pulls her off. The man steps back and the other man walks over and my father pushes him also. Grumbly-grumbly. It starts raining.

I stop flying.

He sticks the second man with a fork. He leans against the chair and his shoulder is bleeding onto the table. My father picks up Ryan and runs from there. The first man runs into the back. She backs up against the place where they drink. She's crying. He sees me and yells come on. I do.

It's raining. It's pouring. The old man is snoring. All the cars there have sticker flags. Yellow ribbon thingies and sticker flags. Red, white, and blue. You can see them in the flashes and rain. I want a sticker flag on my forehead. He starts the car and we back up with her still there. My brother is crying and holding his arms out. But then we're too far away to see her.

The Stained Glass

This stained glass—unlike the others of this sanctuary—depicts a saint of, historically speaking, recent times. Some wonder how a world of trains and factories can possibly give rise to a saint. This stained glass of Saint Elizabeth Bayley Seton illustrates the answer to that question.

If you notice, in the center of the work Saint Elizabeth is holding a book in one hand and a broom in the other. Perhaps you are wondering if Elizabeth was a janitor or a maid. No, not at all. The broom in her right hand symbolizes the inner personality of Elizabeth—that of uncompromising piety, and in addition, her zealous conversion from the Anglicanism of her childhood to the Catholicism of her adulthood. The broom symbolizes how Elizabeth swept her life clean, how she began all over again.

Elizabeth Seton was an individual of tremendous willpower, equipped with poise and grace in the face of daunting change that would have caused most of us to crumple under the pressure. Take, for instance, her husband William's terrible bout of tuberculosis. In New York Saint Elizabeth noticed that he was weak, feverish, and coughing frequently. Soon after the doctors confirmed the worst: her husband had TB. She was, of course, devastated. Around the same time, Elizabeth began a journal, in which she recounted, in horrific detail, her husband's suffering. I must say, in parts of the journal, it is as if Elizabeth was almost scientifically intrigued by her husband's bodily decay (she notes, for instance, the precise shade of his skin from day to day, the precise tinge of his bloody sputum). Yet, she often fell into bouts of depression, cursing God Himself for putting her through such an ordeal.

Soon after, the Setons decided to travel to Italy, partially to visit William's old friends, the Filicchs who owned a merchant house just outside of Milan, and partially to renew William's health. As you know, the Mediterranean was infamous for "curing" those with TB. So the Setons left their four youngest children with relatives, bringing along only their oldest child, Anna Maria. Though the sea voyage was long and arduous (taking over forty days by ship), the Setons hardships were just beginning. Unbeknownst to the Setons, a yellow fever outbreak struck New York City right after their departure. So what? You may ask. Though they didn't have yellow fever, upon their arrival to the shores of Italy the Setons were promptly hustled off to the quarantine station at the port of Genoa.

You see, the Setons operated under a common American delusion, that those abroad will treat us as we treat each other here in the states. In other words, they expected their social class and status as Americans to give them immunity to such trivialities as border regulations. Instead, in this case, everyone's hands were tied. Even Elizabeth's half-brother—who worked in the Filicchi establishment itself could not do a thing. William's health, in the meantime, drastically declined in the unheated station. His coughing bouts took a turn for the worse. As a result, Saint Elizabeth suffered severe bouts of depression, pulling her hair out, and screaming in her sleep. Elizabeth's journal at this time is a harrowing read, filled with passages of expletives directed towards the Italian government and terrible accounts of Anna Maria's attempts to amuse herself in whatever manner she could—chasing rats, eating her own hair, throwing clumps of feces against the walls of the quarantine station. The only peace of mind for Elizabeth was her own growing religious devotion. For instance, at this time she began praying five or six times a day for her husband's well being. Do you see the roses there, rising along the border of the stained glass? They symbolize the horrific suffering of this period in Elizabeth's life.

Finally, the Setons were released from the quarantine station, with only the most cursory apologies from the bureaucrats of Genoa. They traveled inland to Milan, but William suffered mightily. Elizabeth described him in one journal as the walking dead. Several days after their arrival at Milan, William died in front of his wife and daughter, murmuring of visions of angels. Saint Elizabeth was distraught, especially considering a woman's place in society in the early 19th century and the prospects she had for maintaining the welfare of her family. She retreated to reflect upon her future, fasting and praying continuously. Finally, after days of speaking to nobody but her daughter, she decided to return to New York.

If you gaze far into the background of this stained glass, you will see a ship. Do you see that? This depicts the return voyage from Italy, not the outbound journey. Why, you may ask, did the artist of this work chose to represent the return voyage as a part of this stained glass? The answer to that question is the key to understanding the sainthood of Saint Elizabeth. On the return trip from Pisa a member of the Filicchi family, by the name of Antonio, a devout member of the Catholic faith, accompanied Elizabeth, at first just comforting her, then as they became closer, instructing her in the sacraments: the Eucharist, baptism, penance, the rites of the confirmation. Once she reached dry land, she was a Catholic, officially converting on her first day in New York.

Saint Elizabeth's family was, of course, horrified. They considered Catholicism to be the religion of the poor, and looked down upon the complex series of rituals and liturgies we take for granted. Many in Elizabeth's own family scourged her name, and some say her father disowned her for the conversion. Elizabeth's diary reveals a stark portrait of a woman undergoing a life-changing trauma. The fact that some among her family called her a fanatic, even delusional, only strengthened Saint Elizabeth's determination. The week after her father apparently disowned her, Saint Elizabeth served her first communion in the church of St. Peter, surrounded by the impoverished and the profane. This began Elizabeth's intimate relationship with the poor, whom she deemed as worthy of salvation as herself, and whom she found to be far kinder than her selfish though well-to-do family.

Elizabeth only stayed in New York for a few more years, during which time she was able to convert her young niece Cecilia Seton. For this, her family barred Elizabeth from all social occasions. Elizabeth, a woman who was recently widowed, who ran a boarding house to manage, was not allowed to attend any family gatherings, as the Setons were afraid she would proselytize, attempt to convert the entire family to Roman Catholicism. Still, Elizabeth won many smaller battles. For instance, rather than suffer the indignity of exile in the West Indies, as her family threatened, Cecilia came to live with Elizabeth, indeed became her life-long companion. Through the city legislature, the Seton family declared Elizabeth a public menace, and even after Elizabeth's death Cecilia fought and succeeded in removing the title from her aunt's name.

Shortly thereafter, Saint Elizabeth received an offer from Reverend William Valentine DuBourg, President of St. Mary's

College to come here to Baltimore and run this exact school, the first Catholic girls' school in the state. DuBourg included in the offer free tuition for Elizabeth's sons at the boy's school. Saint Elizabeth took the offer, leaving in the middle of the night for Baltimore. This is the more recent history, as I'm sure you are all very familiar from the texts we asked you to study.

So, let it be known that our glorious school has an equally glorious history, and that to become a member of this community you will always walk in Saint Elizabeth's footsteps. Needless to say, soon-to-be-freshman, we hold extremely high standards. You do not necessarily have to achieve sainthood to be successful here, of course. However, martyrdom never hurts.

Amazonia

Richard Long would probably deny the whole setup, but it happened. I'm telling you.

He was the head Newbie, a hunk's hunk. Five foot two and one oh three pounds. Nancy goes for the exotics—the men over five feet five. But ever since the Amazonian Tide, I don't see why we should hatch them any bigger than the mandate.

But Richard was worth a makeover or two. Heather was Kitsy Mongrel last night. Sharon was Treena Robel last week. I wanted the *Sunday's with Susan* Star Phillips job. Boobs that just don't quit. Legs that run from Tuesday to Saturday. Lips the size of a peach pie.

No problem.

After one hour I *am* Star Phillips. Then, I think, how can I really impress Richard? A bottle of nitro? A day-trip to Centurion? I knew he wasn't a star guy. No, I decided to buy him a minute. At the trade kiosk all they had was p.m. slots though. I decided on 9:31. Still, very much in range. Believe me, it wasn't cheap. This would garner some real duty, some real high class devotion. Even years worth.

I put him down for seventy hours a week. A nice mid-range number, I thought. All the slaves were doing at least sixty-five those days. But I didn't want to overtax him. Then I'd have to start all over, ditch Richard in the body dump and begin from scratch. No, seventy was fine, I thought.

I looked at my watch, still had an extra forty minutes of me time. So I got a nice Coke tat on my right tit, a GM tat on my left. They would pay in spades, as long as I could maximize visibility. The slaves would take a good look. How could they not? In the end it they always pay for themselves.

As I walked down the promenade, I thought of the possible repercussions. The worst that could happen to him would be promotion to foreman. The best would be an eventual liberation slot. But as far as Richard Long was concerned, I knew there was far too much fun to be had still. His track was my track for years and years and years.

Passing

I try to tell them it's not complicated, Eddie, but they don't listen to me. I do understand they only have my welfare in mind, but it still bothers me to no end. I know what I want, what I need, but they always *press*. Why, just yesterday they brought me two house plants, even after I told them I didn't need any more. They were nice plants—a cyclamen and a prayer plant, but that means I have to water them. I have to *care* for them. A woman my age only contains so many sparks. I give them hints, but they don't understand that I'm in bed by eight and by eight thirty it's lights out.

Tomorrow I pass you, and that, more than anything gives me the willies, you know. I'm not afraid of going, not at all. But how can I ever be *more* than you when all my life I have been less? I'm sure they will bring me cake, and balloons, and presents, and the kids will come over and plaster a smile on my face. I can't help it. They can't help it. Still, it's depressing, isn't it? I don't think of myself as *old*, and I never have. In my mind, I'll always be twenty-eight, the year we had Kimmy, the year we bought our first home.

Come closer, so I can embrace you, so I can feel your warmth next to mine. Nobody understands like you do. You comfort me and I'm content. This is the only thing that works. They don't understand, you *are* still here. How could I "move on?" There's no reason to.

I have a confession to make. They tried to set me up with another. Two actually. I know this is also what you wanted, but the first was Shirley Waldorf's widower. Looking at his gaunt face, all I could think of was her. We swam in the same community pool for years. We ate hamburgers together at the cul-de-sac parties. He smiled at me and tucked my hair behind my ear, but I can only think of him as Shirley's. The second man I didn't know, but he looked exactly like the guy at the cafeteria. You remember the older gentleman—dapper, always wore the cap and the bow tie? I couldn't take *him* seriously, could I?

I know they are trying to help, but sometimes they don't listen to me. They bring boxes of zucchini and tomatoes and cukes when I no longer eat that much. They bring flowers as if I'm dying. They bring candles and videos for what purpose? I don't need these things.

Last week Kimmy kept asking about a cat. Do I want a kitten? Maybe a guinea pig. Perhaps a fish. She thinks a pet will keep me happy, provide me company. It just seems like too much work, too much hassle. They think more life will ward off death, but it doesn't happen that way. I just want less work.

Today was perfect though. Nobody called. Nobody needed me to take them anywhere. It was too hot to do a thing, but that was okay. I watched the cardinals and wrens gather at the feeder. My hummingbird came by to visit. I ate tomato sandwiches and peaches. I know certain people pity me; I can see that in their eyes. But it's better to be alone and in good health than in an old folks' home. Staying home is all I want. I can't drive. I can't. I get turned around anymore. I feel like a stranger at the mall now—even there. The bumping music, the bright clothes, the movies, computers. I don't understand any of it.

Eddie, when you aren't here I turn the television on. I want the noise. Otherwise, silence is overwhelming. I close the doors to every room but the kitchen and our room. When you aren't here the nights are so *trying*. It's too much space, yet I never leave. So many friends and family are gone. Everyone I grew up with. Most of the people I see on a regular basis I either created or I helped to create.

You have comforted me today, and I'll wait for you again. Only *you* understand my insides. Hold me closer, that's it. You are my better half, still, no question. Even tighter. As tight as you can until the sun burns the night away.

Russet

January

Keith Tuttle always wanted to live in Washington, D.C.; he wanted to share quarters with powerful people. Keith wasn't concerned with climbing the ladder particularly. He didn't aspire to *be* powerful. But Keith imagined himself living amongst the men and women who controlled destinies. He imagined Washington awash with brusque efficiency and order and accomplishment. He thought this would rub off on him somehow.

After saying goodbye to friends and family, Keith packed his belongings in a trailer and hitched it to the rear of his station wagon. His parents watched him pull out of the family driveway, their hands clutched around each other's waists. Keith drove east on Route 80 well under the speed limit. For two thousand dollars a month Keith rented a one-bedroom apartment near Capitol Hill. Though he hoped to find a place with a view of the capitol dome, he settled for one shrouded by trees and overlooking a liquor store. From nine in the morning to eleven at night he could witness the comings and goings of the liquor store patrons. He could hear the bottles breaking. He could hear the fights.

Keith began searching for a job. Though he studied American history in college, he hoped to find a position as an editor of a trade magazine, something simple. He wanted to *enjoy* his free time in the big city. After two weeks and eight interviews, he was hired as a copy editor. His duty was to pour over the minutia of each article, to make sure each piece followed the magazine format.

February

Keith felt as if he was making progress at work, and socially, also. His boss told Keith that his attention to detail helped the association make impressive strides. Keith enjoyed the focus his job afforded him. He appreciated the fact that he was not expected to take his work home with him on the weekends.

Through a colleague Keith met several women, and Keith began dating. Trisha was a hotel concierge at one of the best hotels in the city, but Keith thought she was too mousy, too self-contained even for him. Gina was a bartender, and though Keith found her engaging and energetic, she constantly wanted to "go out." Keith told her he couldn't "keep up."

Keith was not in a hurry to find a life partner. He knew it would happen eventually, and Keith was willing to allow his life to unfold at its own pace. Evenings he watched the comings and goings of the liquor store patrons. On some level he could relate. Habit.

March

When Keith spoke to his friends and family they said they missed having him around. His mother told Keith that she still cooked his favorite breakfast from time to time. "Good thing your father likes bacon and waffles," she said. His mother told Kevin that Keith's father even splurged on a new fancy waffle maker. Keith told his friends he would return for a visit in the fall. "Sure," they said. "You need to get yourself established out there first though. We understand." Keith knew that when she said "out there," she meant "in the big degenerate city." He heard the tone. He didn't mind.

Many evenings Keith would take walks around the mall, admiring the museum facades. He liked to surround himself with the Capitol Building, the White House. Keith rarely felt an urge to go inside the museums. Even if the nights were chilly, Keith didn't mind. Washington winters were nothing compared to the ones to which he was accustomed. In Washington the wind seemed to rarely blast and gust as it did at home.

Keith usually ate alone at the Chinese restaurant or sometimes he bought a sandwich at Schnitzer's Deli on the way home. He enjoyed the feeling of walking home, his dinner in a black plastic bag. The black plastic made Keith feel as if he carried a secret parcel, and he enjoyed knowing that passersby might wonder what he carried.

April

Keith was not ready for the influx of tourists. Growing up in Nebraska, he had heard of the National Cherry Blossom Festival, but he was surprised at how many people actually flooded the city: Germans, Japanese, French-Canadian, Italians, Americans from across the country. The traffic stalled. The Metro was clogged.

At work Keith's attention strayed. Jerry, his immediate supervisor, remarked that Keith seemed to make a sudden rash of mistakes. Keith received an e-mail from Jerry indicating that perhaps he should take a day off.

On Keith's day off—a Wednesday—he attended a session of congress. He wanted to at least take advantage of the opportunity to witness democracy in action. On that day Congress debated a bill on education reform. After an hour Keith found himself dozing off.

That evening for dinner he took himself to an Italian restaurant and ordered pasta primavera with a glass of cabernet. Tis the season, he told himself.

May

Keith went on a date with Karen, a woman who moved to Washington from Kansas City. She was toothy and tall with a bob that made her neck appear even longer than it was in actuality. As a result, her body seemed improbably stretched. They immediately hit it off. "Kansas and Nebraska aren't that different," she said. "Have you ever noticed people don't talk about the Midwest here? It's just flyover territory to them." Keith nodded, and they both ordered chocolate mousse.

Karen worked at a local law firm as a paralegal. She said the work was dull, but that her *entire* life was not encompassed by her career. Keith agreed with this philosophy. When Karen made love to Keith, for a moment Keith found himself moved. In the dark he blotted his eyes with the corner of a blanket. Karen asked Keith if something was the matter, but Keith said it was allergies.

"They are terrible here aren't they?" Karen asked. "I can't take it."

At work Keith found himself in a daze. He would read article after article, but he didn't see the point in correcting a semi-colon, or identifying a missing comma. Who cares? At lunch Keith would walk around Constitution Avenue, gazing at the gray buildings. Even though Keith knew the buildings were no higher than the Washington Monument, the facades seemed to loom over him. Keith felt as if he couldn't breathe. He needed to see the sky, not just scraps of it between buildings and trees. On his computer Keith changed the wallpaper to a rolling russet plain with a clean view of the horizon.

June

When Keith was fired, he felt as if he took it well. He realized his copy editing was half-assed at best. Despite his initial excitement about the position, he just couldn't rally enthusiasm for the level of minutia required. Keith felt too dreamy, too lost in thought. He just wanted to *be*, not to *do*.

Even with Karen, Keith found that he *wanted* to be ordered around. He didn't want to have to *choose*. Keith let Karen choose the restaurants, the movies, which park they strolled around on a Sunday afternoon. Often, Keith was bogged down by the intense humidity; he didn't feel like moving away from the window unit air-conditioning in the kitchen. Keith dragged his mattress to the living room, where it was cooler.

When Karen said she was surprised at Keith's lack of ambition, Keith did send out several resumes. However, he was not invested in the process. He knew he had bills to pay, food to purchase. He just didn't seem to have a preference one way or another. Karen told Keith that though she cared for him, she hated to see him waste his life. "This is a cutthroat town," she said. "But *I'm* not cut-throat," Keith said. "That's just it," she said.

July

When Karen called off their relationship, Keith was hardly shocked. He knew she lost respect for him; Keith couldn't help it. He was who he was. When the heat abated for a few days, Keith did send out a few more resumes, but nothing much seemed to happen. It seemed as if the entire city was on vacation, though the liquor store was still busy. The humidity seemed to amplify the sounds of clinking bottles. The wilted tourists took over the streets. One week Keith didn't leave his apartment once.

His friends and family in Omaha expressed concern. Keith still didn't really know anyone in Washington and he didn't have a job. They asked what he was doing out there. He said maybe he was waiting for something to fall in his lap. Maybe he was lazy. "I do like it here," he said. He wasn't sure if he believed his own words, or if he just wanted to.

His mother told Keith about the renovations the city was making to the waterfront. She told Keith about the beautiful hike she took with Keith's father on the Lewis and Clark Trail. She told Keith about the new flamingos at the Henry Doorly Zoo. Keith felt a place in his stomach tighten.

August

To cover his rent and expenses Keith's parents sent a check. On a sticky note Keith's mother wrote, "For one month only, hon." For the first time in years Keith felt anxiety. He sent out a flurry of resumes and even received two interviews. However, the best he could find was a temp job filing papers for an insurance company at eleven dollars an hour.

Keith thought about calling Karen and asking her if she knew of anything. Keith thought that might show her he had initiative, but he knew his definition of initiative and hers were too far apart. He didn't want to seem desperate.

The full-time employees at the insurance company began asking Keith to fetch coffee for them and make deliveries. Though he considered such tasks menial it felt better than sitting at home in his apartment.

September

Monica was just a secretary, but Keith liked her sweet

demeanor. She had a soft, plush face with buttery skin. Monica teased Keith, calling him a bump on a log. Keith always liked that expression. She asked Keith if he wanted to waste his time on temp work. Keith nodded, saying that he has decided that he really isn't in a hurry. The job only lasted a month anyway, Keith said. Monica said she understood. She was from rural Georgia, and said she grew up believing that people who were always in a hurry were not the kind of people with whom she wanted to spend time. Keith passed the litmus test.

When he walked home from work Keith smelled something in the wind. Keith knew the very existence of the wind meant change was afoot. One cannot help change, Keith thought. He noticed the sharper angle of the sun, the honeyed smolder. Keith thought the smell in the air might even be a kind of dryness, a seizing of molecules.

Monica seemed like a long lost sister to him, a woman who possessed some kind of inside knowledge. Keith wanted to tell the truth around her. He wondered if she thought the same. At night Keith ate Chinese takeout from a plastic bowl. He sat at his kitchen table and watched people enter the liquor store and leave with bags and boxes clinking. He liked the motion. Keith thought of the liquor store as his personal wind chime, constantly circling.

October

Keith didn't know exactly why he was packing the trailer, but then he didn't believe he had to know. His mother said she was elated, and his father said they would throw him a welcoming home party. That was enough encouragement for Keith. Monica told him she'd miss the company. She asked: who else will listen to my complaints about Washington?

Once Keith had disassembled his apartment and packed his trailer, he walked across the street to the liquor store. He walked into the store and found a bottle of red wine. He wanted to tell the man behind the counter that he had been watching the store for months; he wanted to say that he had always wanted to go inside the store but that he was too shy. Keith decided against saying anything. He didn't want to seem like a stalker.

Inside his apartment Keith opened the bottle of wine. Sitting on the floor, Keith drank long swings from the bottle. He stretched his legs in front of him. Keith liked the crinkled feel of the paper bag around the bottle. Keith almost felt as if he were getting away with something. After a while Keith inserted the cork back into the bottle. He tossed the keys on the kitchen counter, turned off the lights, and locked the door behind him. Keith wedged the bottle in between the door and the passenger seat of his car. Keith felt as if he hadn't driven his car in years. When he pulled away from the curb he didn't feel a knot in his stomach. He didn't feel a thing. Keith knew that pretty soon the monuments and buildings would recede. The people he knew and met would withdraw disappear. He knew fields lay ahead of him, brown meadows. That much was certain.

Out at Wakefield

There was a time in my life when tennis was my job. When I say "job," I simply mean it was what I *did*. I'm not a pro, and I wasn't then—not even close. I'm a solid 4.0 player, that's all. At the time I was an unemployed bureaucrat, out of work for seven months.

The lay-offs weren't sudden. I worked for five years as a copy-editor at a trade magazine. Non-profit. Salary just enough to cover the bills and allow me to sock away a few grand a year. Our grants dried up, our funding ran out. The higher-ups didn't want to let us go, but they did. I thought of it as ballast. They had to ditch twenty-five percent of their work force or risk going down with the ship.

My last day with ITPT was in March. The sleet pelted me the day I brought my belongings home in generic white cardboard boxes. The sleet pinged against the cardboard lids as I carried them inside. The ice melted in small puddles in the foyer of my modest townhouse. One thousand seven hundred square feet. Three bedrooms.

For two months the white boxes sat in my foyer. I couldn't bring myself to pick them up, much less open them. I just pretended they weren't there.

The funny thing about being unemployed: I had vast expanses of time to myself, yet this was the most painful part. It was March—chilly, flurries, gusty. The first week all I could do was sit around and watch my old movies on videotape. Something about watching these grainy flicks was a comfort. The color seemed washed-out. The hair was big and out of style. I just let the films bleed into each other.

I ate vast quantities of Orville Redenbacher's, drank Canada Dry to settle my stomach. After two movies the day would still only be half over. Now what? I'd think. Now what? I organized closets, donated old clothes that no longer fit me (the sedentary life sure puts the pounds on). I cleaned everything I could clean—the refrigerator, the bathrooms, scoured the floors, organized and reorganized the filing cabinet so many times I had each piece of paper memorized. There was just only so much I could do. No wife present, no kids here.

I felt useless.

Coming across my old tennis racquets in the hall closet was something. I lifted one of my old Wilson racquets, fingered the white synthetic strings, and held the grip in my hand. I used to be able to hold my own, never able to beat the top seeds, but always consistent, nettlesome, a smart player. I only stopped playing because my knee gave out—had to get arthroscopic, lay off it for a long while. After I lost my mobility I just felt as if stepping back on the court would be a losing battle. I couldn't accept a lesser version of myself.

But holding my old racquet gave me, somehow, the impetus to at least whack a few balls around again. What else did I have to do?

The first day back was rough, let me tell you. Mid-March, windy as hell, I'm out at Wakefield Park trying to gauge my toss and serve. The net seemed huge—the size of a barn. The service box seemed tiny. The wind took my toss behind me on one side, two feet in front of me on the other. Still, I hit four hoppers of ancient balls—even if only a third of them went in. I had Wakefield Park to myself.

For a week that's all I did—practice serve. Hopper after hopper, until finally I got my timing down.

The next week was calmer, warmer. I decided to work on my groundstrokes. One of the many aspects I love about Wakefield: aside from all the courts, they have six fenced-in sections of hitting walls.

When I was a young high-school player I used to play imaginary matches on the wall. Wilson Duke versus Jimmy Connors. Wimbledon final. Back in those days I really let 'er rip.

Post knee operation I only had enough coverage to stand in one place and hit forehand, forehand, forehand. Then backhand, backhand, backhand.

The ball thumped against the wall, and then bounced on the cement, and then thunked against my racquet strings. The sounds. The beautiful sounds.

Several weeks later I had established a routine. I'd serve for an hour, with drink breaks after each hopper. Then I'd work on groundstrokes for an hour, with frequent drink breaks. Finally, I'd practice volleys and half-volleys for fifteen minutes.

By one o'clock—when I usually wrapped-up, I was pooped and hungry. I'd eat two hard-boiled eggs, a toasted hamburger bun, and some applesauce. Then I'd take a nap.

This way I felt useful, more useful at least.

I met David the first week of April. Though I'd occasionally see a doubles game in progress (retirees) or a few college kids working on their strokes, at eleven in the morning the courts were deserted. A usual cadre of 4:00 to 6:00 players came hell or high water—sleet didn't faze *them*—but mornings were dead.

Dark eyes under his taupe baseball cap. Long and lanky. Young kid, I thought, maybe twenty, twenty-one. I watched him hit against the wall for a few minutes. He was athletic, quick, if a bit ungainly. I'd guess he began playing within the last two years.

"Hi, there," he said, leaning over to pick up a scuffed practice ball.

"Hey," I said. "Strokes are looking good." I didn't know what to say. I felt old and pathetic. I also, for some reason, wanted a cigarette.

"Thanks," he said. "You wanna hit? I mean, do you have a partner?"

Did I "wanna hit?" That was a good question. I did *want* to. Whether I *could* or not was the question—at least without embarrassing myself in front of the young gazelle. But… I told myself: you've been working hard at your game; the serve is coming along. You are striking the ball. What is all this for if you're not going to at least hit the ball back and forth with a real person.

"Sure," I said. "Why not?"

At the time I had a son David's age. Still do. Frank. Franklin. He lived with his mother in California. Silicon Valley, where my ex-wife's new husband, Hunter, was employed. Still is.

I raised Franklin until he was nine. I was a good father, as good of a father as I could be. His mother turned religious—born again. She said unless I did the same she'd divorce me. She couldn't "have intercourse with filth," she said. I was, seemingly, the filth. During the divorce proceedings she accused me of child abuse—spanking—and influencing Franklin toward a life of drugs: we watched half a Cheech and Chong movie one afternoon. The judge was somehow swayed by her lawyer. End of story.

I have tried my best over the past nine years to maintain a relationship with Franklin. Difficult three thousand miles away. Even more difficult when his mother has home-schooled him, isolated him, told him I'm "poison" as far as she's concerned. Franklin seems ambivalent at best.

I do the expected duties—send cards, gifts, make the occasional phone call. I've visited him a few times—this is allowed—though I hate California with a passion, Silicon Valley most of all. In the end it doesn't matter. Hunter is his father figure now. I'm peripheral at best.

David and I stand at our respective baselines hitting the fuzzy yellow ball back and forth. Not much drama in practice, though I can tell within two minutes that David will need some guidance. This doesn't make me happy. I've always disdained the pomposity of the few self-anointed Wakefield tennis mentors. Just because you like to talk doesn't mean you're wise.

Still, as David slices backhand after backhand into the net, I know his form is off. So is his mind. The forehand looks okay, I think, though his backswing is far too long and loopy. Who knows? Maybe he's just getting slopping because we're only practicing. Still, I can't move. This is a problem.

There's only one way to tell.

So after taking some volleys and overheads and giving David a ration of the same, I ask him if he'd like to play some games, maybe a set.

He flashes me a wide grin—ear to ear. Good, competitive guy.

"I'd like to," he says. "But I need to go in five minutes. Have to be some place."

"Okay," I say. "Another time then."

I thought he was just blowing me off, but five minutes later he comes to net, shakes my hand, enters my phone number in his cell phone and says he'll call me.

"I'd like to play sometime," he says.

I didn't think he *meant* it. Just thought he was being nice. Never expected a call. Two days later, however, David called me.

"Would you like to hit some tennis balls?"

"Sure I would," I said. "Hell yeah."

We meet out there at Wakefield. David is leaning against the green electrical box, a plastic bag of balls in one hand, his racquet in the other. A small water bottle juts out of his sweat pants pocket.

We go to court six, adjacent to the meadow and walking path. It's my favorite court—pastoral, green, open. Court six is filled with light. I crack open a new can of balls.

"Here's to good tennis," I say. "Maybe great tennis."

I flipped two balls to David, pocket the third. It was sunny and crisp, about forty-five degrees. In a month I knew the courts would be busy with activity. That day we *owned* the courts.

After warm-ups I asked David what he does for a living, what he's up to.

"I graduated from JMU a few years back. Unfortunately I majored in art history. Doesn't exactly open doors. So right now I'm delivering pizzas," he said.

"Okay," I said. "Good." I told him at least he has a job and that I was without one, hadn't even sent out my resume. I was afraid he'd ask me if I wanted to deliver pizzas—he didn't.

"It's good for my tennis though," he said. David worked nights.

We played mediocre tennis that day, at best. David seemed like a smart kid, but he went for too much on half his shots—tried to blow it by me. He hit most long, or into the net. We didn't play a match that day—just hit and then some practice points. He was adjusting though, trying to. If he kept at it I knew he could only get better.

Mentoring is a lost art, I thought.

Tennis was my job. Barring rain, I showed up every day—practiced serves, hit against the wall, hit with David or an old timer if one came along. I put in my time.

I played with David on Tuesdays and Thursdays, and we began drilling, working on the subtle points of his game. I taught him to stay down on his backhand, to shorten his strokes for control. We worked on his serve—"pretend it's a fishing line," I told him. "Snap your wrist for power." We worked on the mental facet of the game—knowing when to go for a winner, when to keep the ball in play, when to lob, when to hit an intentional short ball, to draw his opponent to net.

Working on his game helped me focus mine. By late April we were playing ten-point tiebreakers. By May we were playing sets.

David got frustrated quickly. I'd win 6-1, 6-2, but only because he made so many unforced errors—two, sometimes three a game. "It's difficult to overcome that," I told him. David would slam the ball into the fence, bash his racquet against the net, curse, scream—all those silly McEnroe antics that plagued the game when I was growing up.

I told him to keep his composure—even if something went wrong.

I tried to listen to my own advice. I sent out my resume.

By June I still hadn't landed a job, but I did receive several interviews. This was encouraging.

With each passing week David's game became stronger, more consistent. I couldn't move well, so David's speed helped him immeasurably. He got to *everything*.

"It's so demoralizing to hit a winner—what I think is a winner—and then suddenly the ball is coming back."

His frustration level subsided as he came closer to winning sets (4-6, 4-6).

We stood under the shade of an elm tree during changeovers, drinking water and Gatorade. David chewed gum.

"I'm moving in a few weeks," David said.

I felt as if I had just been doused with ice water.

Oregon—not as bad as California. But still… I thought. But still. He was moving out there to live with his sister. She thought she could help him get a teaching job.

"That's great," I said. "Really."

Most nights I'd collapse in front of the news by ten. Wake up at five thirty and repeat. The last time David and I played I let him win a set: I admit it. I'm competitive, but I wanted the kid to go off thinking he'd progressed. He had. I couldn't think of a better gift.

For dinner I sautéed ground beef, mixed that with rice and beans and onions. Lived off that for three days or so. I still can't look at ground beef in the same way now.

David gave me his e-mail address and told me he'd keep in touch, keep me updated on his tennis progress. I didn't expect him to, and he didn't.

I went back to my steady diet of hitting against the wall and practicing my serve. I found a few new partners, also; there are always tennis partners out there. Always more.

In early August I landed a position—more editing for another non-profit. I must be a glutton for punishment, but I still have the position. Haven't played tennis in weeks.

A New Cycle

Each dog has its corner. The two brothers sit back-to-back in the middle of the room, feet out. Crab-like. The brothers smell of sweat and shit. Their clothes molder against their backs. The snow quickens on the slats high above.

When the men come, the dogs eat and drink from the metal trough. Whatever the dogs don't eat the brothers get. Slim pickings. The brothers gnaw on bones.

They try to forget the night. The accusations are just that— accusations. They know their morals are sound, no matter what. When the dogs glower, it is difficult to remember this.

The dogs sleep and wake from sleeping. It is as if they take turns. The men come and rotate new dogs into the chamber, relieve others. The dogs have clean fur, and they smell of pastures and pinecones.

"How long have we been here?" the younger brother asks. The dogs lift their heads, and one lifts its mouth to snarl, then doesn't. The older brother taps the younger brother.

"It is nobody's concern," he says. "Concentrate on faith."

Easier said than done, the younger brother thinks. The older brother closes his eyes. He remembers the days when the sun would slant through the windows, when the sweet, lilting music carried over the water. Those were days when their mother would stand them up, brush their hair, whisper.

The dogs don't pant. They hardly seem to breathe. Their eyes are waxy, ringed with the same gray in the granite walls. It will go on like this.

VI.
ARS
PROSETICA

The Mirror

Jordan Schuster hated mirrors—"the providence of the vain," he said. If he *did* glance into a mirror it was merely to watch the slow path of his razor when he shaved, to avoid nicking his Adam's apple or gouging his upper lip. As he shaved, Jordan's wife Glenda would often circle his waist and rest her chin on the spot where his shoulder and neck meet.

"You just look so handsome," she said. "I couldn't ask for a better husband."

Jordan usually shrugged her off, stating that if he never had to shave again he would be delighted. He would gladly sacrifice eating and sleeping as well—if he could—devote his entire energy to work. Jordan's only ambition in life was to bask in the glory of his authorship, the entire reading public with a copy of a Jordan Schuster novel tucked under their arms.

When Jordan asked Glenda for her hand in marriage he told her that his only caveat was that her life with him could be lonely, that his true calling in life was not family, or children, or love. His literary ambitions ruled the roost.

"I want to be the most influential writer of my time," he said. "Nothing less will appease me."

"Then I will be there to accompany you," Glenda said. "Your

journey is my journey." She said she loved him unconditionally, that she was a lucky woman.

Glenda never complained about the evenings she spent alone, reading or sending letters to friends while Jordan wrote in seclusion. Jordan would go for days without thinking of his wife at all. Often Jordan would only speak to his wife in the morning when he awoke, and at meals. Otherwise, he locked the door to his study and told Glenda he just would not be disturbed. Glenda was young and beautiful and showered Jordan with love, when Jordan allowed her. As Jordan would have it, their lives were simple, spare, uncluttered with children or dinner parties or grand events. Occasionally, when Jordan was exhausted from his work, the couple would attend a play or dine at a restaurant, but these were mere diversions, and in the back of his mind Jordan continued to ponder his plots and characters. Glenda was nothing more than a pleasant distraction, Jordan thought, a human condiment.

As Jordan grew older the success he had hoped for seemed more and more elusive. Publishing houses went of business. The editors with whom he was acquainted moved or died or retired. Though Jordan published a collection of short stories, the minor press that published it quickly folded thereafter, and the few reviews that his book did receive were mediocre at best, published in marginal magazines that folded themselves within a year or two. This discouragement only made Jordan more determined. This only sparked in Jordan a greater fire to achieve his goals. Jordan began writing for twelve-hour stretches, day after day after day after day. He wrote books without stopping, compulsively constructing plots and honing dialogue and developing complex character motivations. One book bled into the next. He sent his manuscripts to the publishers that remained, becoming increasingly shrill and desperate in his correspondences.

Though Jordan noticed the worried look on Glenda's face, he also knew that she supported him, that she wanted him to succeed and would do whatever it would take to allow Jordan's ambitions to reach fruition. Glenda began staying up late with Jordan, serving him tea, massaging his shoulders, helping him to bed when he collapsed at his desk in sheer exhaustion. Lines of unease began forming on Glenda's beautiful face, and her hair began to gray.

Jordan's few solitary friends told him that he should take a vacation, enjoy life, allow himself to recoup. While Jordan knew his body could certainly use a break, he couldn't stand the thought of wasting time. He *had* to finish his next book first. This book will be the one that will bring me into the public eye, Jordan thought.

Two weeks later Glenda became ill. Suddenly she could no longer raise her body from bed, and she began coughing violently, racked with chills and fever. Glenda said she only caught a cold and that Jordan needed to return to his work. Though Jordan had to make his own tea and fix his own toast, he knew he would survive. When he returned to bed that night he found Glenda curled into a ball under the covers, skin blue, teeth chattering, a cold sweat upon her temple. Jordan was suddenly alarmed; he drove his wife to the hospital as fast as he could.

The next day Glenda slipped into a coma. A week later she was proclaimed brain-dead, a virtual vegetable.

Jordan was wracked with guilt and shame. At his wife's funeral Jordan stood silently by her casket with a bewildered expression upon his face. Her friends and neighbors and relations told Jordan that Glenda was so beautiful, so patient, so understanding, such a warm and giving person. What a tragedy, they said, an absolute disgrace. That day Jordan floated, as if through a dream.

Returning to his empty house Jordan felt rootless. For weeks he sat at his desk, staring at blank paper, unable to conjure up a single word. Though he wanted to continue to write, he couldn't. Jordan couldn't concentrate. As soon as his thoughts returned to his novel, they strayed once again. Months passed, then years. Jordan was frozen in a void, unable to do anything other than eat and sleep and gaze with a clenched stomach at old pictures of Glenda, radiant, pure.

Eventually Jordan hired a housekeeper to perform the duties that Glenda once did. Though Betsy was competent and kind, Jordan resented her and hissed at her for the slightest mistake or oversight. Jordan's shoulder's hunched inwards and he began to spend most of his time in the bedroom, reclining with the curtains drawn, sleeping late into the day. He bolted his study, unable to set his eyes upon his own writing.

When Jordan Schuster died, his younger brother discovered Jordan's manuscripts locked in his study. Since Jordan's will failed to specify what to do with the manuscripts, his brother tossed them into file boxes along with Jordan's notes and correspondences, stowing them away in a crawl space. They donated Jordan's yellowed copies of his one and only book to the city library, but the librarians shook their heads and apologized: they lacked space on their shelves for a single one.

Simple

Aaron and Rebecca live in a ramshackle, 30s era, bungalow just outside of the city proper. Their squat home consists of two bedrooms, a living room, a lean railroad kitchen, a bathroom, and a musty, dirt floor basement. They bought the house on foreclosure three years ago, but Aaron doesn't hold a paying job. Rebecca works erratically, mostly temp slots. Neither Aaron nor Rebecca has health insurance, savings, or retirement. Aaron considers himself a writer, though he writes infrequently. He usually sleeps until eleven, eats, showers, flips through his porn magazine collection, checks the mail, does an occasional crossword puzzle (if it's not too difficult), then maybe, if he still has the energy, writes a bit until Rebecca comes home. Aaron would prefer revising to writing. He likes to refer to Flaubert's quote—the one about a good day's work consisting of a well-orchestrated paragraph. Aaron can't recall exactly how it goes. But he likes it if Rebecca is at home his motivation to write actually increases. Aaron feels additional pressure to do *something* productive. Rebecca reads over his shoulder, reads each page. Aaron feels a warm wash of gratitude for Rebecca, his wife, his motivator.

Nine months ago Aaron and Rebecca stopped paying for heat and electricity. With the money Rebecca makes temping they can barely cover the mortgage. Aaron has worn out his welcome asking his parents for money on numerous occasions. They try to limit their food budget to $40 a week. Rebecca is good at finding ways to cut corners—canned fruit, day-old bread, lots of au gratin (parmesan) pasta and frozen dinners. To save money Rebecca prepares their meals on a camping stove and hibachi. They eat from paper plates with plastic utensils. They eat in candlelight. Simple.

"I'm wondering," Rebecca says, her voice trailing off. Rebecca feels an inordinate burden. If she goes to work she worries about Aaron's writing (or lack thereof). If she doesn't she worries about money.

"Yeah," Aaron says, poking at the Spaghetti-O's. "This is actually pretty good. Especially when you mix it around some. The tastes come out."

He watches her shadow loom against the wall. Her head and shoulders bleed over the plaster.

"What if *you* work? I'm just saying you might take fuller adv—"

"Advantage of my time."

"Yeah, you know, focus on the hours you have afterwards instead of, you know..." Rebecca is ruddy-faced, flaxen-haired. Her hair spills out of its bun, cascading over her ears. Aaron thinks of Rebecca as earnest, as a straight shooter. Rebecca knows she possesses a buried maternal instinct; she would do anything for her husband. She is an *optimist.* Aaron knows Rebecca believes in her and that, as a result, he needs to give something back.

"It's not something I can do," Aaron says, wincing.

"Just a thought."

Rebecca says she doesn't want to nag. Aaron says they've had this exact conversation before. He's a writer. That's his job. If the world doesn't want to *reimburse* him for his effort, that's not his problem. He puts in his time, Rebecca says. You do.

Aaron is tall and lean and scraggly. His eyes are the palest blue, the color of Windex. His face is long and equine, giving him an exotic look. He presents himself as a gypsy, a Gallic troubadour. In Aaron's MFA program he was known as "Boccaccio." Aaron's MFA program was the highlight of his life—a time to revel in writing— thinking about writing, talking about writing, finding "his voice." His mentor, Sterling Brown, a bawdy National Book Award nominee, advised Aaron to live a "consciously chosen bohemian life," to avoid the tortures of the nine-to-five life. "The drones!" He emphasized life choices, paring down, simplifying. "Whatever you do, avoid work," he told Aaron. "You need wide swaths of leisure to write, to create. Months and months at a time." Aaron feels indebted. Simple, simple. Yet, sometimes he wonders if this was good advice. For him.

Aaron is often unsure if he has found his voice. He lives a "bohemian life," or at least he thinks he does—he buys his clothes from a thrift store and both he and Rebecca are conscious vegans. He drinks obscure craft beer, always. He e-mails his MFA comrades on occasion. Otherwise, Aaron is alone with Rebecca. Rebecca is all I need, Aaron thinks. He has to admit to loneliness though. He *is* lonely. Jaded. His thoughts often stray from writing. He wonders if he was meant to be a writer or if it is just another pretension with which he protects himself.

When Rebecca remembers their justice of the peace wedding she thinks of Aaron's mustard-colored shirt, his thread-worn khakis, his tattered green and pink striped tie. Aaron didn't cry—his face was fixed in a stale expression of ambivalent neutrality, as if they were at the DMV waiting on a new license plate. The tarnished ring he bought at the pawnshop was sufficient. It would do. He stood there staring at the ring as if it were a worthless and unlikely object—a pebble, a bottle cap, a bent paperclip. Shitty. Yet they were happy; they were together, an island unto themselves. Islands in the stream, that is what we are, Aaron thought. They were high school sweethearts. Aaron and Rebecca were inseparable. Simple, simple, simple.

When Rebecca does work Aaron calls five or six times a day. Every slight detail is worth hashing out. Every infinitesimal decision is worth a discussion.

In the morning they don't read the newspaper. Instead, they talk about each other's dreams. Aaron has a recurring dream that he is a fire breather in a circus in the Amazon. Aaron has another where he weaves rugs in an Egyptian caravan. Rebecca dreams she is a water spider, giving birth to thousands of spider babies in the middle of a vast desert lake.

In January the temperature dips into the teens; it snows; it's dark. The experiment without heat or electricity begins to lose its appeal for Aaron. It's difficult to do anything swaddled in thermal underwear and sweaters and blankets. No crossword puzzles. No porn. No writing.

Instead, Aaron *thinks* about writing. He runs short story ideas through his mind. Aaron realizes he's only written three short stories since last January. At this rate it will take him five years to finish a book. This, he thinks, is a piss-poor level of production. Aaron feels creaky and old, even at thirty-two. His MFA friends are publishing books. He's published two measly stories in crappy online magazines; as a result of his poverty and lack of electricity, he often can't even read the stories from his home.

Unless he goes to the library and Aaron has never enjoyed

walking into libraries—he has always felt the expectations from all those books pressing down on him, intimidating him. Bullies. But from the frozen wasteland of his home the local library suddenly seems as comforting as a mug of hot chocolate.

Sick of the cold and the dark, Aaron showers, dresses, turns the ignition on his rusted-out Camry. He calls Rebecca as the car warms up.

The snow banks strike Aaron as somehow medieval, reminiscent of ramparts on some Scottish castle. I need to practice stepping-up, Aaron thinks. Be a man. Aaron realizes if he lived in a prior age he might be deemed a eunuch at best, perhaps a male witch. Artists are always outliers, he thinks. Still, what's the benefit? Aaron feels cold and alone. Both feet on the ground, Aaron thinks. Both feet on the ground. It sounds like the title of some insipid self-help book. Still, Aaron knows this is what he needs.

Aaron parks the car in the half-empty library lot. He lets the car engine idle, warming himself in the heat. He calls Rebecca, tells her he loves her, tells her everything. Then he shuts off the engine, walks inside the library to the computers. The library is warm, and the computer glow a comfort. It has been a long time since he has looked at a computer screen. He re-reads his two published short stories. Then Aaron scans the classifieds. He does this for a long time, sitting in front of the computer, scrolling up and down the white screen.

The Last Novel

F is a writer who dislikes other writers. F prides himself on the fact that other writers find him brutish and "unliterary," though he knows he is neither. F wears the armor of ironic disregard. He dresses in sweatpants. F loathes literary affectations: "Who is your agent? Who is your publisher? Who is your publicist? If I may ask, what was your advance?" As far as F is concerned, they can all jump off a cliff. On other days his fantasies are more vivid. He'd rather sit in a room, write. He'd rather sit in a room, read. He'd rather talk to his very unliterary friends, drink a beer, watch television, walk the dog, stir fry broccoli, reupholster the couch, wash his car, and check the mailbox. Anything but talk to other writers.

F is writing a novel entitled *The Last Novel.* He has been writing this novel for twenty years. F's novel is 22,387 pages long. The novel is so expansive and vast and all-consuming it contains a mélange of additional novels. It contains all plots and characters simultaneously—at least this is F's intention. F has already included over nine thousand, three hundred various characters. F imagines his novel to be the last word in novels, the final statement, the swan song of novels. He hopes that after reading his novel, writers will cease the practice of writing novels in awe of his accomplishment. Abandon hope all ye who enter! Drop your pens!

F is an optimist. Not only does he believe his project is doable, he is positive it is. In addition, F is searching for a computer programmer who can formulate a program, based on the logic of *The Last Novel*, which will allow the novel to continue to write *itself* after F's death. F's ultimate ideal is that *The Last Novel* will never reach completion. A complete novel is a finite novel, and a finite novel is one which can, one day, be surpassed. As a result, F has never sought publication for his novel, for publication would entail utter failure of the project. It would entail completion. Giving up the process.

F avoids literary events at all costs—readings, writers' happy hours, book festivals. It's all a waste of time, F thinks. He doesn't want to listen to abstruse drivel about the "nature of internal language." He doesn't want to discuss his own writing, his "voice," the "lyricism" of his work. F considers himself a *doer*, a man of action. If he could he would hole himself in his study every day, all day, pump nutrients into his arms so he wouldn't have to move. F doesn't want a vacation. He doesn't want rest. He just wants to write, to continue the development of his infinite novel. Continuously. 24/7/365.

Still, F has a wife. G is patient with F, doting. G understands F's ideals, and even if F avoids showing G his manuscript, she smoothes his hair down, massages his shoulders, tells F that if he needs anything he should ring the bell. F keeps the bell in his desk drawer. In a previous incarnation it functioned as his mother's dinner bell, and before that his grandmother used it to spook the spirits from the corridors of her Roanoke farmhouse. G also writes. G primarily writes haikus and tankas, though she doesn't do this often. When G does write she immediately commits the poem to memory. Later, as a means to help F fall asleep, G recites her poems. She does this with a breathy voice, and while she recites the poem she smoothes down F's hair. F likes having his hair stroked. He admits this. He doesn't mind admitting this.

One day G wants to attend a reading. Two of G's haikus were published by a local literary magazine, and she hopes to recite them in honor of the magazine.

"*Why?*" F is not looking at her. He is looking at the computer, typing, clicking, typing, scrolling.

"I'd just like to share bits of myself with the world. I'm curious."

F proclaims it to be an utter waste of time. Why not just write instead? That would be more productive, more worthwhile. "Readings are insipid," he says. "They cater to audience passivity."

"You don't have to go," G says. "Don't go."

F lifts his eyes from the screen. G's face is cast in a blue wash. Her mouth constricts. The skin of her eyelids seem thin, veiny. F doesn't *mind* being married. If it weren't for G he would need to work much harder to maintain his basic, bodily functions. If it weren't for G, he wouldn't' be able to support himself. His life would consist of work and drudgery. F is grateful, but he realizes he doesn't always *act* so.

"I'll attend," F says.

G blinks and clasps her hands at her waist.

When F was a boy he imagined married life would be saturated with duties and in a sense F put-off his proposal to G for years for exactly this reason. Yet, because G was his high school sweetheart, he was unsure. F lacked curiosity in other girls. He knew he *should* maintain an interest in them, but he didn't. F never thought of the suburban life as inherently boring or out-of-touch. F was easily amused, interested in the day-to-day.

The reading is held in a boutique furniture store, which also houses a café/coffee shop. To F the store offers the appearance of "hipness," urban funkiness. The furniture is retro, upholstered in purposefully garish hues—rust, pumpkin, lime-green. A woman with black-rimmed glasses and a pre-Raphaelite mane of curly locks offers a drink to F and G. A table sits adorned with humus, crackers, feta, pineapple cubes, and grapes. She introduces herself as the editor. A gaunt man with a rust-orange sweater leans against the wall, judging. A woman in a scraggly, puke-green and yellow-striped shirt bugs her eyes out at F. A tall, gangly woman with jet-black hair circles the room, staring.

"I need to sit down," F says, and he does. F hunches in the far corner, staring at the exposed brick. He traces the mortar from left to right. The mortar makes a perfect grid, F thinks. The wall is mathematical. The lines extend into infinity, F thinks. *The Last Novel* is this wall, F thinks.

As the reading begins, F is lost in reverie. He imagines ways in which he can develop various characters and plot-lines and descriptions. F races through an incomplete mental list of words he has not yet incorporated into his novel. He aspires to use every word in the English language in the last novel. He *must*, in fact. Yet, even with over twenty two thousand words written, the task (and many others) seems daunting. I am the wall, he thinks. The reader changes—the voice seems familiar. F imagines pages and pages he could write. He has so much to capture.

"How did you like my reading?" G says. She is holding F's hand. He hadn't noticed. Did G read? It was a blur. This is what happens to the mystics, F thinks.

"What demon possessed me that I behaved so well?" F thinks. Who originally said that?

"Wonderful," F says. "Visionary." G squeezes his hand, and

when the reading ends they walk outside into the early winter air. The sky seems pregnant with impending snow, F notices. F almost always notices the sky.

"Feels like snow," G says.

"I was just thinking that," F says.

And if G wasn't holding his hand, and if they weren't climbing into their car, and if F weren't a human being at all, but a pure stream of energy, an electronic impulse, F would, at this moment, be content with his lot. As he watches the first sporadic snow flakes, he knows, in the end, he will have to be anyway.

The Miniaturist

The miniaturist paints miniatures of miniaturists drawing miniatures. To do this, he sits in his one room cabin in the woods. The room is surrounded by larch and beech and twittering green birds with dangling ochre wattles.

From his cabin the wood smells of something forgotten. Some distant age. Quills and parchment. Latin.

When darkness descends, the miniaturist will lean over the fire and heat his evening meal—potatoes, beans. He will eat it with exact movements of his mouth—back and fourth.

He doesn't miss the grandeur. Softness and words are a memory. His children have long since misplaced him. Or he has misplaced them. This is the way.

When morning comes the miniaturist will rise from the floor, and sit at his desk painting miniatures. The leaves are an incandescent green. He hasn't allowed himself under them since the trees were bare. That was when the woman came to him. When he ordered her to. That was long ago.

About the Author

Nathan Leslie's nine books of fiction include *Madre, Believers,* and *Drivers.* His previous book of stories, *Sibs,* was published by Aqueous Books in 2014 and his novel, *The Tall Tale of Tommy Twice,* was published by Atticus Books in 2012. He is also the author of *Night Sweat,* a poetry collection. His short stories, essays and poems have appeared in hundreds of literary magazines including *Boulevard, Shenandoah, North American Review,* and *Cimarron Review.*

Nathan was series editor for *The Best of the Web* anthology 2008 and 2009 (Dzanc Books) and he edited fiction for *Pedestal Magazine* for five years. He is also currently co-editor for a fiction anthology, *Shale,* also published by Texture Press. His website is www.nathanleslie.com and check him out on Facebook and Twitter.

www.ingramcontent.com/pod-product-compliance
Lightning Source LLC
Chambersburg PA
CBHW030403020726
47493CB00003B/926